INFINITE
METROPOLIS

Chrysalis Award-Winning Author

EDMUND SCHLUESSEL
AND MIKKO RAUHALA

Infinite Metropolis

© 2020 Edmund Schluessel and Mikko Rauhala

www.aurelialeo.com

Schluessel, Edmund and Rauhala, Mikko
Infinite Metropolis / by Edmund Schluessel and Mikko Rauhala

ISBN-13: 978-1-946024-85-5 (ebook)
ISBN-13: 978-1-946024-86-2 (paperback)
Library of Congress Control Number: 2020931743

Editing by Zelda Knight
Cover and Interior illustrations © Gabriel Santin
Book design by Samuel Marzioli |
marzioli.blogspot.com

Printed in the United States of America
First Edition:
10 9 8 7 6 5 4 3 2 1

Edmund S: For Samantha, still making her escape.

Beyond this gateway between universes, you will find what you seek: a newly improved metropolis built by the brightest minds in the Milky Way! However, do not allow connections to our past to impede the progress towards our future. It is imperative that we focus on the task at hand. Otherwise, why are we here? We encourage all newcomers to face New York City with fresh eyes and engaged minds. Welcome to the Deepened City citizens of Earth! We hope you enjoy your stay.

— SPONSORED BY THE KOLLAN SOCIETY FOR MULTIVERSE COOPERATION

THERE ARE AN INFINITE NUMBER OF STORIES IN THE NAKED CITY

EDMUND SCHLUESSEL

Ray smoked a cigarette on his balcony and looked up. There was no patch of sky visible amid the tower blocks above him but he imagined a tiny dot of gray at the limit of his vision. It had been raining earlier, and rain had to fall from somewhere.

He flicked the ash from his cigarette over the railing. Somewhere at the bottom was a street. He hadn't liked going down there. The street stank like piss and whatever garbage people left on it. Now, ever since the city deepened, he didn't have to go. When Ray went to work the elevator took him eighteen floors up to the M stop, the M–most of the signs still said "subway"–took him a hundred blocks south to the office complex, and if he needed a drink or a movie or some groceries he could stop someplace in Midtown on the way back. Sunday off, then Monday back at it: stability, predictability, exactly what the pro-Deepening campaign had promised was here.

He looked up again. Some other Ray, God knew how many floors up, was thinking these same things, smoking the same cigarette, wearing the same faded blue jeans and sleeveless undershirt. Once in a while he even saw the flick of cigarette ash from maybe a thousand or a million floors up drift by, followed a few minutes later by the spent butt.

He turned his head left, right: the view the same in every direction, skyscraper after skyscraper after skyscraper, floors and floors of humanity, electric lights in windows going on forever. Ray's cigarette, his own little ember, was finally spent so over the edge it went. As Ray leaned over the rail, the abyss sprayed him with vertigo. There was a tickling little voice in his head, at the limit of hearing...

No. Not in his head. It was the voice of a young woman, echoing from below off the sides of the skyscrapers, maybe from miles down.

"Hello? Hello? Is someone up there? I'm lost!"

No reply came from above him and nothing from below. Fuck it, someone had to answer. "Hello? Where are you? I can't see you!"

"I'm on the street! A Hundred and Forty-Fourth and Seventh! I can't see you, what floor are you on?"

"I don't know!" As Ray answered he realized the voice from the street should know that was a dumb question. The deepened city started at ground level and went up forever. Nobody knew what number floor they lived on.

Shit. "Lady, you're not from the city, are you?"

"I'm from North Dakota! I was visiting my cousin and I got stuck in the hospital! They said I was out for a month!"

That explained it. The city had deepened three weeks ago. The Mayor had boarded a balloon over Times Square and pushed a button and just like that, Manhattan parted ways with reality. Ray, like most New Yorkers, had decided to stay with the city (the Bronx and Long Island didn't count. Staten Island *really* didn't count). He'd stocked up on cigarettes, written a few e-mails to some distant family, and life went on.

"Lady, you missed out on a lot. You know we're in another dimension, right? You can't get out!" If you crossed First Avenue West, you came out on the east side of a new copy of Manhattan from an imperceptibly different quantum reality. Same if you tried to cross the Harlem River—you'd end up in Battery Park. In the run-up to the Deepening, all the buildings had been heightened to an equal 1,776 feet so their top floors could connect to the second floors of their copies. Ray didn't know what would happen if you tried to go down a manhole, but it couldn't possibly be good.

"Someone at the hospital told me there's a way out! Walk through the Holland Tunnel! But my cards don't work anymore and I don't have any money! I need to get out on foot!"

The Holland Tunnel? That was a hell of a thing. What did they charge for tolls now?

"Listen, if you're going to the Holland Tunnel, you wanna go north! That means the big street number going up! Then you'll cycle around again and keep going until you get to Canal Street! You got that? North! Then west! North then west!"

At the faintest limits of hearing, an echo without words. Oh hell, she was crying. The woman's words came up muffled from the street. "I've been trying. I just keep going in circles. I keep walking north and I end up on Wall Street again, over and over."

"I dunno what to tell you, lady. Listen, if they can get in through the Holland Tunnel, won't your husband come get you or something?"

"He doesn't even know I'm here!" Ray knew the rest of the story before she said it. "I was meeting a man! Carol! And we went to a hotel and did some coke. I took too much. When I woke up, he was gone and I was in the hospital all alone... What have I done? What have I done?" Millions of people could hear her but hardly anyone could see her. The Deepened City was a good place for anonymous confessions.

The sobbing from below faded into silence and Ray thought the woman had gone. He realized he missed the voice, so instead of going inside, he called, "Lady?"

She was all cried out, winded from crying. There were exhausted breaths between the phrases of her words. "Mister, you're the only person who's really talked to me in days. What's your name?"

He took a breath. "Ray!"

"I'm Henske!" Henske. Hell of a funny name. Memorable, at least. The air was still. It had been still a long time. "Listen, Ray! I need help. Can you come down and walk me to the Holland Tunnel?"

That was a hell of a question. Ray was about to tell her no when he heard Henske again.

"Oh, I'm so grateful! You don't know how grateful I am! I'll wait right here for you! I'm wearing the floral print dress and the yellow sun hat!"

Ray realized he'd been talking to an echo. Some other Ray, the one closest to the street—"Famous Original Ray," he'd called his downstairs copy–had answered Henske. He was picking up on the dregs of the conversation that started miles down. Well, he was glad some other version of him had been willing to help. Henske sounded pretty... Fuck it, somebody had to help.

And that someone is me, thought Ray, as he started packing a backpack with food and water and a couple of packs of smokes. He'd go down to the street and see if she was still there. If she wasn't, maybe he'd catch up with her at the Holland Tunnel. Maybe he'd get out of Manhattan and back to the world.

And if he met another couple of Rays along the way, hell, they could team up. They knew where they stood with each other.

Ray slung the backpack over his shoulder and closed the balcony door. He'd left a note for any other Rays that might stop by on their way down–the apartment key would work, after all–telling them to help themselves to whatever was in the kitchen. If he'd heard Henske, he couldn't be more than a mile or two from the street at most. The others would have longer trips. He stepped into the hall and closed and locked the apartment door behind him.

He never saw the falling man dressed in blue jeans and a sleeveless undershirt who passed his window at terminal velocity a few hours later, or the one that followed a ten seconds after that, or the one ten seconds after that, each one in successive states of grim desperation, terror, rigor and decay until an ossuary mound piled from the street at One Hundred-Forty-Fourth Street and Seventh Avenue toward the invisible, unreachable sky, striving forever to escape.

THE PETER PRINCIPLE

EDMUND SCHLUESSEL

C heck my hair. Is it alright?"

"It's fine. You know, Mr. Wackerle likes it straight; you should've straightened it."

"I'm not going to change my hair for that little twerp, yeah?" Macy sucked her teeth in annoyance. She knew Tracy had a point, but not losing herself had been hard enough at the beginning.

It was even harder now that the firm had hired Tracy. Tracy's name was Macy. Macy again. Macy-twice. Tw-acy. Tracy. She was a parallel version of Macy from the next reality over, one who'd been laid off by her version of Macy's firm, and who'd taken a job at the closest alternative that was hiring...

"Look, everything's going to be just fine," Tracy said. "Restructuring happens. This is *your job already,* hon. That makes you the strongest candidate." The two of them had a pact. They'd flipped a coin to decide who would apply—it took four flips; they both called heads the first three times"—hey'd split the salary difference so both of them would get the same amount of money.

"You're right," Macy replied. "I should try to relax." She took a breath and tipped her head back, allowing her eyes to drift around the car of the M. As she adjusted, her Grandma Nell's brooch on another woman's lapel, and matching blue pantsuit, caught her eye. Macy nudged her duplicate.

"Hey, look at that! Someone's wearing the same outfit as me." Then the image clicked, and she focused on the passenger, her face framed by straight, highlighted hair, Macy's own face. A third one of her.

Tracy nudged Macy. "Don't stare, hon." She'd been staring too. "I bet she's interviewing for our job."

"Oh damn. Damn damn damn..." Macy repeated.

"Don't let it get to you, hon. She's just doing what we'd do. Just pretend she's not there, go in and give the best interview you can."

The M slowed to a rough stop, and Macy and Tracy—and the third one—all got up and made for the elevator plaza that led to Donatello & Hayes's corporate office.

It took the first twenty floors of their eighty-floor ride for Macy to say something.

"So you're interviewing for the..."

"Right. My version of Donatello & Hayes, well, we went under. We're closing down, so..."

Tracy rushed off the elevator on the seventy-seventh floor and left the two of them alone.

"Oh, that's, that's, are you okay? Like, is the apartment..."

"Oh, the apartment's fine, it's just, you know."

As they left the elevator on the eighty floor and entered Mr. Wackerle's reception area, the office door opened and a sandy-haired man Macy didn't recognize stepped out, not looking at either of them as he left the waiting room, his right hand shaking in a tight fist.

"At least *that* guy isn't getting the job," she said to the new Macy—Macy-three? Thracy? No—. It stopped sounding like a joke as soon as it wasn't in her head anymore. The third Macy's laugh was more of a cough.

Then Don from HR stuck his head through the door, and as it turned on its hinges he called, "Ms. Macy Garland? Ms. Macy Ga—oh my!" he exclaimed, throwing up one hand in forced cheer. "I guess we should just flip a coin!"

•

"I dunno what to tell you, Macy. The other Macy just wanted it more." Dan Wackerle's accent was pure West Texas, but his heavy sweating revealed why he came to New York City. However, since the Deepening, the Infinite Metropolis was eternally summertime, and the air conditioning was out again. "How could the interview team possibly be biased against you, anyway? You look just like her, and you have the same resume as her..."

"What am I supposed to do, Dan? I've been here for *ten* years, and you *know* I've got rent due, right?"

"Macy. Macy. Shh, shh, shh." Mr. Wackerle shook both hands, palms down. "We'll take care of you! You can stay in accounting!

You and Tracy'll just both be back to junior."

That was six thousand dollars less a year, but it was enough to live on. She shook her head but said, "Alright. It's something."

"We need you to move your things out of the supervisor's cube too." Wackerle was pressing on despite Macy's capitulation. Maybe she could set her new desk up next to Tracy's?

•

"He's a liar," Tracy said to her later while they packed up Macy's desk together. "It's the hair. He hates cornrows."

Macy bit her tongue, too hard, to hold back the lump in her throat, and went to find a quiet room. "If anyone asks where I went," she said to her duplicate, "tell them I'm going to look for boxes."

•

"This dehydrated reconstituted par-boiled vacuum-converted crystalline *shit* we get in the City now is barely worth calling coffee," Tracy complained.

"Yeah," Macy replied, "but I still want to get it right. Gotta have something to take pride in."

"Hon, I hope you don't think this is your niche. We're management material. You know it."

"Yeah, Darcy is." Macy-*thrice*, Thrice-cy. Darcy. "She's a suck-up."

"Don't be so hard on her, hon. You know she's just what we'd be if things were a little different."

"She's an easy girl to work for, I guess?"

"You know that e-mail this morning? From garlandt3 to

garlandt and garlandt2 about looking in a folder? Did you look in the folder, hon?"

"Yeah. All set up so it would make sense for us. It'll take us like an hour. I'm gonna do the coffee run, Tracy."

Macy smiled for Mr. Wackerle as he topped up his "#1 Uncle" mug, smiling even bigger when she served coffee for Darcy. Milk and half a sugar, just like they all liked it. Big grin. No eye contact.

No eye contact with the two new Macys either. They never talked. One brushed her off every time Macy made an overture. The other one had haunted eyes, with dark circles beneath them. Macy had heard a whisper from Tracy about the woman who was just garlandt5 on the office e-mail list—"out of work for a year."

Today, though, Darcy broke the customary silence. "Rumor upstairs is we're moving to new offices farther uptown. Cheaper."

Macy made a noncommittal "hm" when she heard the words at first, but as she walked away from Darcy's desk, let out, "I suppose I'll just sleep less."

Mr. Wackerle stuck his head out the door as Macy traveled to the break room. "Hey darling! Can I get a top up?" The "#1 Uncle" mug was empty already. Macy realized this was the big Texan's sixth cup before noon.

"Gotta shake this headache, I think I'm tired or something." Macy topped up the mug with thin black coffee and made for the elevator even as Mr. Wackerle muttered an inattentive "fankoodarln." However, before she reached the elevator doors, she heard a loud thud behind her. She turned to see it was Wackerle on the floor, purple-pink. When Macy turned him onto his back, blood was dripping from his left ear onto the floor.

Response times for first aid were hell—the system couldn't decide whether to route the call up, down, north, or south, and it took two minutes for an operator to even pick up. Macy gave directions and prayed she was talking to an operator from the same copy of Manhattan.

•

"Doesn't anyone get time to grieve?" Tracy whispered as she drummed her nails against the plastic frame of a cubicle. "It's only been a week."

Macy shushed her but wasn't sure why. The whole office shuffled from foot to foot in Mr. Wackerle's former reception area. "They're all thinking the same as me, right? I mean, they have to be." Half the department was Macy Garland. She'd heard there were one or two in other parts of the office too.

But she never saw any of them other than Tracy in the break room. She never saw anyone else in the break room anymore.

Don from HR—did he even have a last name?—strode into the room with a decades-obsolete clipboard under his arm. He raised it and clapped both hands over his head. "Welcome, everyone! Thank you all for waiting. I'm very happy to introduce to you the new department manager!" If he'd been around eight hundred years ago, he'd be blowing a trumpet with a banner on it.

And there she was, the new manager, yet another hungry external hire from an accounting firm somewhere in the Infinite City that had gone bust, or maybe just someone climbing the ladder and seeing an opportunity in someone's death.

She was wearing such a deep black suit her skin almost looked pale, speaking with a cloying, attention-seeking emphasis. "Hell-ooo, everyone! It's so nice to be here! Sorry if I don't introduce myself, a-ha-ha-ha-ha... You can call me Nellie." Don laughed along with the new boss. Nellie. Macy Nell Garland. It was handshakes all around, then back to work. Macy tuned out the small talk, but when it was her turn, her new manager —"Say hello to the new you!" Tracy had quipped. "Don't call her that," came Macy's retort, with anger that caught her by surprise—smiled and shook her hand and with a sentence, Macy knew she was trapped forever: "Oh honey, you're bringing everyone down, do something with that hair!"

THE GRAND HOTEL
MIKKO RAUHALA

The doorbell of the Lawrence residence rang just as the family had finished saying grace at the dinner table. Well, Trevor had finished, anyway. Sarah was simply playing along, but that was fine. Marriage was made of compromise, of going along with one another's idiosyncrasies.

"Shall I?" Mark asked in a squeaky voice. Embarrassed, he covered his mouth with his hand. His breaking voice hadn't stabilized yet.

"I'll get it," Sarah said. "You two have slaved over the dinner quite enough." Trevor's janitorial job at their building allowed him some flexibility with his working hours. It came in handy when it came to looking after Mark—their son—as well as fixing dinner.

Sarah walked over to the apartment door and cracked it open. She gasped when she saw another version of herself standing in the hallway, dressed in a familiar long, blue overcoat covering a lighter blue office dress. It was the exact thing Sarah had worn when she'd come home after a hard day's work at the department of continuum engineering.

There would have to be a pretty good reason for another Sarah—what would she even call her? Sarah? Mrs. Lawrence? Sarah Prime?—to show up on her doorstep. Trevor wasn't very comfortable with the Deepening. It was messing with God's creation. If worlds were meant to be together they wouldn't have been created apart, that sort of thing. Still, he'd stuck through it, stuck with her. Sarah—any Sarah—wouldn't want to rub the new world order in his face unless it was important.

Prime's expression was grim, though she tried hard to put up a brave face. She gave Sarah a little wave. "Hello, Sarah. It's fine, you can call me Prime. It is your home, after all," she said meekly.

"Umm, okay. Hi. Prime." She glanced behind her.

Trevor was peeking in on them from behind the corner. His brow furrowed. "I'll just go close the kitchen door so we can talk in peace," he said. "Mark, we'll be a moment. You can continue with your dinner."

Sarah turned to face the visitor again. The kitchen door closed behind her, and Trevor's footsteps returned to the corner. He kept his distance.

"So, what brings you to our floor?" Sarah asked, tilting her head.

Her brave face crumbled in an instant. "There was a bombing near ground level. Some anti-Deepening terrorists trying to bring the whole thing crumbling down. They failed, obviously, but I didn't know what to do. My family... My family..." Prime stuttered with a trembling voice before breaking down in Sarah's arms.

Sarah stroked the back of her crying counterpart while glancing at Trevor. He wasn't hiding his uncomfortable cringe very well.

"Okay, it'll be okay," Sarah repeated automatically, not sure if and how she meant any of it. "Come on in, we'll talk this through."

"Ah," Trevor said. "It's just... this sort of thing could confuse Mark. Of course, you—*we*—should help... her out, but could you perhaps take it outside?" he pleaded.

Sarah's eyes narrowed, but she didn't turn to show him. *Hiding behind Mark, of all people.* "Fine," she said with just a bit of ice in her voice. Then she addressed her counterpart again, noticeably warmer. "Let's slip into the stairway. Half a floor down, yeah? Have a little talk there?"

"...yeah," Prime managed, detaching from Sarah and walking towards the staircase. Sarah followed, closing the door behind her. Trevor could damn well take care of himself.

The Sarahs sat down on the stairs by the half landing. Sarah wrapped her arm around Prime's shoulders.

Prime sighed deeply, taking a moment to compose herself. "So I suppose the three-body solution is out of the question then," she said quietly.

Sarah laughed hollowly. "Glad to see you haven't lost your edge. But yeah. You know Trevor. It's not likely to win traction with him. Still, I thought there was an obvious way out, given that you know that you're not the only Sarah around. We were basically the same person until the incident. Little would have been lost if you'd just—"

"I know, I know. I'm still down with pattern identity theory, but it turns out that actually killing yourself is *really hard* even if you have a timely backup."

Sarah nodded. "I suppose you never really know until you're face to face with the prospect."

"No. You don't. Mind, speaking of, could you..."

"Eh, sorry, no," Sarah cut Prime off. "Turns out we're not killers either."

"Thought as much. Given all that, you know why I'm really here, right?"

"Yeah. The Trevor and Mark in my apartment are patterned like yours, thus they are, in fact, the same people," Sarah said.

A hopeful glimmer lit up in Prime's eyes. "Right. Should make sure that we're otherwise in sync, though. You did the routine checks on the integrity of the spatial splicing at work today?"

"Yep. Nothing's unraveling. But Roger spat out his coffee when a decimal point had accidentally moved to the wrong place."

Prime chuckled. "That's right. Poor guy thought we were all going to die of imminent dimensional collapse. What about your Mark, did he have trouble with the bully again on Monday? Did Trevor cut his finger while fixing something on Tuesday?"

"Correct. Okay. No reason to go through our life stories; we seem to be in sync well enough, the last few hours aside. This is your floor now. I'll go one level up and do the swap there and so forth, and we can all have our families back."

"Thank you, thank you, thank you, but..." Prime grimaced. "What about Trevor? I mean, he's still my husband to me, but he'd say different. Are we really okay with deceiving an infinite number of Trevors just to help me?"

Sarah closed her eyes and sighed. "He is a bit old-fashioned, isn't he? Bless his heart. But it can't be helped. I wouldn't want to be left alone to grieve were I in your shoes. I won't do it to you either. It's not in me. Besides, it's not an infinite number of Trevors that we'll have to keep in the dark. The moves are not instantaneous."

Prime tilted her head. "That's right! Eventually, old age will stop the swapping front. So, in the grand scheme of things, zero percent of Trevor instances will be affected. I... think I can live with that."

"Just remember to educate Mark on philosophy. It'll help if he's on board in principle, even if we never tell him."

"But it'll be nice to have a sympathetic ear if we'll need it someday," Prime continued, nodding along.

"Right. Now, to catch you up real quick, Trevor complained about feeling a bit under the weather, like he might be coming down with something. And Mark said his teacher had actually shut down the bully pretty good today, though we'll have to keep an eye on the situation."

Prime smiled and started taking off her overcoat. "Got it. Here, you'll need the coat. More to the point, I'll need to not have it going back in."

"Ah, of course."

As Sarah took the coat, Prime grabbed her in a tight hug. "Thanks. I don't know what I would've done if I wasn't such a nice and reasonable person."

"Well, who can you count on to have your back if not yourself?" Sarah said, returning the gesture.

Prime let go and took a few steps back. She and Sarah looked at each other, nodded, and turned away. Sarah proceeded toward the elevators while Prime opened the apartment door to face this instance of her husband.

Trevor was pacing nervously around the living room but seemed visibly calm when only one Sarah entered. "Everything okay?" he asked and raised a curious eyebrow.

Damn, the red eyes and all. "Yes. I mean, it did get a bit emotional, you know. I wasn't quite prepared to meet myself in these circumstances." She wiped her eyes and sniffed. "Might've caught that cold or whatever of yours too."

Trevor softened and smiled meekly. "I understand. I'm not unsympathetic, as you know. It's just..."

"I know. We're worlds apart."

"Right. Will she be okay, though?"

"She'll be fine. She'll be staying with family."

THE HAPPY LIFE

MIKKO RAUHALA

Peter raised his hand to the doorbell, then checked the name on the door again. "Peter Simmons." This was his apartment all right. The same scratch on the door frame from when they had squeezed the couch in, the same missing floor tile next to the door, the same grime in the hole. Even building maintenance was uniformly sloppy across the deepened skyscraper.

He pulled back his greasy hair and rang the bell. For a moment he wondered if the local Peter might be out before he shook his head. Were this a normal day, he would be home, tuning out after a hard day's work by watching reality TV—whatever the hell that meant anymore. The local Peter would be doing just that and shouldn't be too plastered to have a proper conversation.

Indeed, the door opened. "You're earl... Oh!" the local Peter said, taken aback. He was dressed in a neat blue shirt and straight black trousers. His eyes were sharp, and there was no waft of alcohol on his breath.

The Peter who'd rang the doorbell felt self-conscious in his tattered blue jeans and black t-shirt of some rock band he'd never listened to. He didn't even own the sort of clothes this other guy was wearing. "Uh, were you expecting me?" he asked.

Squinted eyes glanced past the arrival into the corridor. "Somebody else, but not quite yet. What's up? Where you from?"

"Downstairs. Look, can I come in? I have a favor to ask, one Peter to another." That was how the Peter who'd approached him had said it. It had been hard to refuse another version of himself when he'd put it like that. Some sort of camaraderie among Peters.

The local Peter hesitated, then stepped away from the door. "Fine, just for a moment."

As Peter entered, he couldn't believe his eyes. The studio was his but wasn't. The piles of trash were gone along with the flies and the sketchy odor. Everything was scrubbed clean, the floors, the tables, the works. The couch still had traces of familiar stains, but he had to know where to look for them. The only thing that was the same was the show on TV, where Alice Twelve was just complaining about Alice Seven hogging all the booze at last night's party. It was good to see that he still had *something* in common with this Peter.

The local Peter turned the TV off, erasing the commonality. "So, out with it," he prodded, glancing at his watch. While it looked cheap, it was something else Peter didn't have. After the essentials— rent, food, and booze—he didn't have a lot left for anything else.

"Um, yeah. Thing is, I was just visited by the Peter below me, and so on. There's been some problems with living near the ground floor.

Trash piling up on the streets from above. Bodies, even. You know, you've seen some of the jumpers."

"Yeah," the local Peter said, his expression grim. It went without saying among Peters that they hadn't always been very far from joining that crowd.

"So, the lowest Peter got fed up with it and decided to move up in the world, you know. Asked the one above him to move one step above, and so forth. Makes sense, right? There's always one more apartment. Nobody has to live near the ground."

"And you agreed to move out of your apartment trusting that I'd let you have mine?" the local Peter asked, his eyes narrow beneath furrowed brows.

"Everybody else has, and we're all the same, so I figured..." Peter cursed inward. It had been easy to move from one identical shithole to another. But somehow this Peter didn't live in a shithole. Somehow, he'd cleaned up his act when everyone below him hadn't. If he were him, he wouldn't be all too keen to let go of his apartment.

"Look, I get where you're coming from, but this here, it ain't happening. You look like crap, and I'm betting your apartment looks and smells the same as mine did two months ago. I'm staying put."

Fuck. "Look, whatever's going on, I'm sure the one above is just as good as yours. Maybe they just keep on getting better."

"Don't try to bullshit yourself. Just as likely I'm the freak among us. Maybe more so. Besides..." He thought for a moment, then he sighed and softened his expression. "Look, Peter to Peter, right? I'm gonna do you a solid. I've got a good reason to want to stay right here. I've met someone, and from the looks of it, you haven't. But if I had a shot with her, you might have one with your version, or the one above, if *you* want to try your luck there."

"Oh?" Peter's ears perked up. Maybe the day wouldn't a total loss. He'd been feeling rather lonely for what seemed like forever, which was funny in its way in a city with infinite people around him.

"Yeah. You know the woman three doors down to the left? I'm pretty sure you've checked her out. I know I had, even before."

Shit. Peter knew exactly who his counterpart was talking about. He'd flipped her off on a bad day last month when she'd bumped into him in the hallway, and things had gone downhill from there. If they ran into each other now, it was a good day if all he got was an icy glare.

"Yeah, I know who you're talking about." He tried to keep an earnest expression but felt like some of the disappointment was bleeding through.

The local Peter raised his eyebrow and continued. "Right. Jane, she's called. I ran into her on the stairs when the elevators had a glitch a couple of months back. We bonded over bitching about it, and one thing led to another."

Fucking butterfly wings. Peter's elevator was the only thing that hadn't been glitchy in the last few months. Now he'd already fucked up his chances with his Jane. Upstairs then? If the Peter there was like him, it'd be the same there. And if he was like the Peter here, that Jane would be spoken for as well. There was only one way this was going to work.

Still, it would be suspicious if he didn't ask. "How would I approach her?"

"She likes cats, horror flicks, and classic rock. That t-shirt is fine but wash it, man. It was pure luck for me that mine was clean. We have pretty much the same sense of humor, so do your worst there. Also, she's coming over soon."

Peter narrowed his eyes momentarily. *Asshole.* "Thanks, man. I'll get out of your hair. Just gimme a glass of water for the road."

The local Peter moved aside and pointed his hand at the kitchenette. "Sure, help yourself." He seemed tense. Did he suspect something? Peter would, but this one wasn't quite himself anymore. It could just be the discomfort of having his less fortunate version intrude on him. He might have let his guard down.

Peter moved in and took stock of the kitchen utensils in sight. The chef's knife would do nicely. He'd get rid of his counterpart, add him onto the piles of cadavers below. He'd figure out something with Jane. Perhaps feign an illness so he'd have time to adjust. This life would belong to him.

When he went for the blade, he felt a crack at the back of his head. The force of the blow slammed his face against the counter. He fell down onto the floor, and the searing pain caught up with him.

Something yanked at his collar, turned his face up toward the dimming lights. A snarling face entered his field of vision.

"You've fucked it up already, haven't you? I haven't forgotten what it was like to be you, *asshole*," he heard as the world faded to black.

REASONABLE DOUBT

MIKKO RAUHALA

Peter yelped as he was pushed into a sturdy chair inside an interrogation room. "Is this really necessary?" he asked in a trembling voice as the officer handcuffed him to the armrests.

"Nah, just what we like to do to murder suspects around here. Isn't that right, Miller?" the officer said to her partner, who was sitting behind his laptop on the other side of the table.

"That's right, Johnson," Miller said from behind a sickening smile. "And going by the expression on our friend's face, we can strike the word 'suspect.'"

Peter became aware of the sudden paleness of his face. *Murder.* The arresting officer had only mumbled something about improper disposal of garbage. Dumping in general was a major offense in the infinitely high metropolis, but these officers had followed through and found out what exactly he'd tossed over the railing. He'd tried to make sure nobody saw him dispose of his murderous asshole of a clone a few weeks back, but apparently, he'd failed. The jig was up.

Not that he'd go down without a fight. Not much reason to, not in a murder case. If the charges stuck, his life would be over anyway. Maybe he could plead suicide?

Probably not, but Peter needed to know for sure. "I'm pretty sure somebody mentioned something about a lawyer. I'd like one now, yeah?"

Johnson nodded. "One has been requested," she said, taking a seat next to Miller.

"Now, the public defenders tend to be rather busy these days. It might take a while..." said Miller, turning his smile down a notch. "You don't *have* to say anything before your lawyer gets here but being cooperative might help your case."

"You're not *necessarily* looking at a life sentence," Johnson put in. "For instance, if you told us, voluntarily, what you had against Jane—"

"What?!" Peter cut her off, his eyes wide open in panic. "Jane's dead? How? When? Why?"

The officers glanced at each other. For a split second, they seemed less sure of themselves, but then they nodded at each other and toughened up again.

"Don't play coy with us, Pete. We have footage of you dumping her body off the side of your building last night," Miller said.

"No, no, no! That can't be! I just saw her this morning, when we'd..." Peter trailed off. Jane had spent the night, but as far as Peter was aware, she'd left for work in the morning as usual.

"We'd what?" Miller asked.

"Lovers' quarrel. Should've known," Johnson said.

Miller snorted. "The age-old story. Look, mister. Every NYPD instance runs randomized drone surveillance, and we share the data to give us a full picture of what's happening everywhere, all the time. Every drone within a hundred Manhattans pointing at your building at around 1:03 AM saw this."

He pushed a few buttons and turned his laptop around. The screen was filled with nine video feeds from different angles. All showed Peter dumping a heavy plastic bag over the railing.

A wave of relief flowed through Peter as it dawned on him. "But... these are all the other Peters! You don't have footage of me! This me!"

"You're as guilty as any of you! There's no version of the feed that doesn't show you doing this. No reasonable doubt," Johnson said.

"But... I'm sure there are; I can't be unique! A hundred Manhattans, you said? Look further!" Peter pleaded.

Miller scoffed. "Multi-Manhattan bandwidth isn't cheap! Every version of you who hasn't been caught on camera will be making the same demand. That said, the Inter-Manhattan Surveillance Ordinance gives you the right to look for your needle in a haystack—on your own dime."

"What! I don't have that sort of..." Peter started but was interrupted by a knock on the door.

"What, the lawyer already?" Johnson asked, visibly annoyed.

Ah. The lawyer. Peter had already forgotten all about asking for one. That had, no doubt, been the point.

Miller stood up and opened the door. Another police officer stood in the doorway. "Guys, there's been a development. There's someone you'd better meet."

A frenzied woman pushed her way past the officer and barged in. "What the fuck is going on here? My Peter's supposed to have murdered someone last night? I'll have you know he was with me the whole time!"

"Jane! You're alive!" Peter shouted. He tried to jump up, but the handcuffs raised the chair up with him, and he crashed back down. Jane made her way around the table and embraced him.

"Jane? The vic?" Miller asked, his tone incredulous.

"Vic? What do you mean?" Jane asked.

Miller sneered and pointed at the laptop, which was still looping the surveillance footage. "The thing is, pretty much all the other versions of your boyfriend here were getting rid of your dead body last night."

Jane stared at the screen, the indignation on her face rapidly melting away. "That's... The bag could be anything."

"You'd think so. But, after being alerted to the dumping, we intercepted the next version of the bag falling through our section of Manhattan," Miller said and pressed an arrow key. A woman's face, beaten and bruised, appeared on the screen. Peter squinted. There was a lot of damage, but the familiar jawline, the strong eyebrows, the mole next to the left eye... There was no mistake. It was Jane, all right.

Jane stared at the image, her mouth agape. She glanced at Peter, then jumped away from him.

"Jane, I can explain! It's not me! I'm different! I love you!" Peter shouted.

Jane shivered, her breathing quick and shallow. "I... I can't..." she stammered. Then, she rushed out of the door.

Miller pursed his lips, rubbed his forehead, and sighed. "Well then, Mister Simmons. If you don't mind, I'm gonna go ahead and cancel that lawyer. You don't seem to be needing one anymore. You're free to go."

Johnson smirked. "Though, you might want to consider couples' counseling."

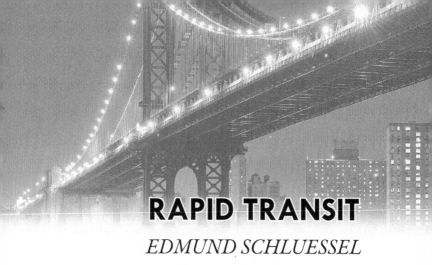

RAPID TRANSIT

EDMUND SCHLUESSEL

Part I

In the time it took to swallow, the old world was gone and Bil was standing on the tarmac at the lip of the Holland Tunne and the heat and the stink of the streets of Manhattan landed a haymaker square in his open mouth.

The traffic warden with the Port Authority badge nudged hin out of the way to make room for the next arrival from Earth. Bil joined the bustle of refugees—a few dozen in this lane—and lookec for his brother.

A figure took shape on the arrival platform, a flat outline gainin; depth as it turned, to the hum of electrical generators. Its outline wa familiar for a split second and Bill's heart clenched. "Aaron? Aaron!" he called as his cheeks tingled from hyperventilation. *No.* It was jus an old man who'd been behind him in line on the other side. The warden moved the arrival into the crowd. The coils hummed again as another outline appeared, and crumpled to the ground, flat and limp as a fallen poster, evaporating into monatomic mist at its edges.

"Incomplete transition," someone called into a walkie-talkie. "Mister Leakey, please update?"

Whoever and wherever Leakey ways, he kept his demeanor level as a test pilot in a crashing plane. "No signal from the other side, Reception." A pause. "No lock."

Bill lunged from the crowd around him, hoping his brother had come in by another lane. The guard put his hand up and pushed Bill back. "Hold on, sir. We'll get you processed, then we'll help you find who you're looking for."

Aaron could take care of himself. Bill tried to breathe evenly.

•

The interviewer had an open-topped cubicle on the tenth floor in a building which had been a ventilation tower when Bill was a kid. She stood at her adjustable desk. "So, Mister"—a glance at her terminal—"Warespoon. Tell me why you felt you needed to flee your home reality."

Bill sat, like the accused in a courtroom. "World ending." Bill shrunk at his own flippancy. He called up more of the memories from the place he'd hidden them. "The asteroid was first, square in the middle of Siberia. That set off all the volcanoes, and those melted the permafrost which thawed out the superplague, but then the Chinese saw a chance to finally get the Russians out of the way and the Russians figured they'd take us all with them..." Vertigo hit. He'd let too much out. When it was UNN hungrily reciting "one billion dead" or "crop yields falling" or "Refugees flood Afghan border" it could be put aside. Now Bill was falling into a dark pit.

"Did you see any of these missiles, Mister Warespoon? Or perhaps an explosion?"

He was back in the steel chair in the cubicle. The woman seemed to have gained a foot in height—or Bill had shrunk. "No, no, I didn't see any missiles, what kind of question is that?"

The woman looked past him, held up one finger and nodded to someone behind Bill's left shoulder. "Mister Warespoon, we need a complete picture of your circumstances for your asylum claim. As I'm sure you understand, enormous numbers of people come here making all kinds of claims…"

"Ma'am, I'm, I'm a U.S. citizen!" The woman's desk seemed to be getting taller still above him, and now the cheap carpet was shifting under Bill's feet.

"If you can produce a valid passport, U.S. birth certificate or other proof of citizenship, Mr. Warespoon, you will, of course, be immediately admitted."

They were back in the world he'd fled. For all Bill knew his Jersey City didn't even exist. "I, I, I… Wait!" The woman peered over the frames of her glasses at him. "Can't you contact some other version of me, from another Earth? I know he'll vouch for me!"

"A parallel version of yourself, sir, would only be able to prove citizenship for himself. It's been four years since the Deepening. A person might have lost their citizenship through migration, renounced it... Sir, I understand this is difficult, but this is a city. We have to manage our resources."

"I..." There was no longer breath in Bill's lungs.

"I think we have to cut this short, Mr. Warespoon. Please register your address in Manhattan Posanetupa with us as soon as you can. The information's on your card. Officer, how can we help you?"

Officer? Bill looked over the shoulder. The blue-clad policeman had been standing there for how long? Bill rose unsteadily as the officer beckoned him into the aisle among the cubicles. Another officer leaned on a pillar.

The first policeman was mustached, pink-faced but somber. "William Warespoon?" Bill nodded. "Mr. Warespoon, I'm sorry, your brother is dead. His body was found in a delivery truck arriving via the Holland Tunnel. We believe he hid in the truck in a pallet full of instant mashed potatoes, unaware that transition through a cargo point would be fatal." The officer was reciting a formula. His mustache barely shifted.

Bill couldn't feel his own body. Even the comforting embrace of air pressure and gravity seemed to have fled.

The other one put his hand on Bill's forearm. "I'm sure it was fast and painless, sir. A couple hundred people every year try to sneak in through the cargo lanes. They never look like it hurt..." The rest of the word faded out and Bill floated through the next hours as a ghost. In the years to come, Bill could remember a coroner's office with white walls and bright fluorescent lighting. He could remember nodding his head and saying, "Yes, that's him," and then he was standing on a sidewalk and the city was all around him again.

The sun had recently set. The line of street lights stretched on forever in every direction. Bill had no money, no identification, and nowhere to sleep. He relied on the grid of Manhattan to guide him and walked east.

•

"I don't need an asylum claim," he muttered to himself as the black of night solidified. "Just get me out of here." A heavily laden truck passed him on his left as the road sloped downhill. "HOLLAND TUNNEL" read the sign above the entrance. On the other side was a still thriving Earth. There'd be another Aaron, someone whose life had been almost like Bill's brother's, except it continued. Adrenaline got Bill into the line at the exit terminal, but he had to force his eyes open while standing in place. The teenaged son in the family ahead of him had writing embroidered on his jacket: "bacon ham, mustard time" and then "fries burger cool" in cursive below it. Trying to figure out what it meant kept Bill awake.

It wasn't until it was his turn he understood the line moved so slowly because guards were taking tickets before letting people through. When they confronted him, he didn't fight—he just turned around and walked out, back to Manhattan. He sat down on the sidewalk. Within a few seconds of half-sleep, he understood what he should have tried. "I'm a fucking refugee," he said to the air around him. "They don't even want me here. Fucking deport me." His head tipped forward and he slept.

Bill awakened to the metallic rattle of a truck stopping suddenly.

The sun was up, and his skin felt like the sidewalk looked: encrusted with mummified garbage and the shit of a million dogs. His ankle itched. He picked himself up and started walking again, without a destination in mind, east again, mile after mile as his empty belly seethed. Manhattan repeated, avenue after avenue: there was never a Williamsburg Bridge. It all started over again with a new iteration of Canal Street. The piles of torn garbage bags, the colonies of rats among them, they were new every time. The rats didn't scatter, even when Bill kicked an overwhelmed garbage can. They had learned fearlessness.

Bill checked his itching ankle. Some lucky rodent had eaten a piece of him while he slept.

He walked faster and changed course. There was one address he knew.

•

"Sir, this is Manhattan Posanetubee. You're registered in Manhattan Posanetupa. I can't help you."

It was the same elevated desk, the same red glasses. This version of the civil servant wore a different pantsuit, but today was a different day.

"Ma'am, I just need someplace to stay while I figure out how to get out of here." Bill held his baseball cap in his hands by the brim. "I'm not even trying to get into the City. I want to go back to Earth."

"Earth Posanetupa is unreachable, Mr. Warespoon."

"It's gone. I told... I told your counterpart."

"For whatever reason." She wouldn't give an inch. "We cannot send you back to your Earth of origin, you are claiming you cannot return for fear of death, that makes you an undocumented migrant seeking refugee status. You are in the system as such." She sighed. "We've got more beds than Posanetupa does. We'll transfer you here." She lowered the desk and printed a smart card on a metal template. "Do not lose this card, Mr. Warespoon. This card is your ID and your only legal access to funds."

Bill closed his fingers on the azure rectangle. The civil servant didn't let go.

"You're not legal yet, Mr. Warespoon. This card gives you a maintenance allowance." A different printer buzzed. "This piece of paper here, these are directions. While your claim is being considered, you may not work or apply for jobs, you may not engage in any commercial activity, and you must remain in the Metropolis."

If Bill could get out, would they send cops after him to deport him again?

"Welcome to Manhattan, Mr. Warespoon. Good luck."

She didn't sound hopeful.

Part II

Five thousand dollars for a ticket back to the world, the travel agent had demanded. Seeking work not allowed, the border control agent instructed. The little sign in the vending machine right below the packet of instant ramen noodles proclaimed "$2.00" in neat block letters.

They'd given him a metal card with a chip and a magnetic strip and told him that was the only money he was allowed. It worked at shelters and a short list of stores—big names. He could cash any value on it in, but only if he was done with the shelters and his asylum claim was granted. *If.*

The first night, Bill had gorged himself on the free dinners the shelter handed out—instant mashed potatoes, water that stank of bromine, and tofu that was fishy in all the worst ways. It was food and Bill was alive, fed, even a kind of clean.

The second night through the fifth, he wept. *Aaron went fast.* It was his only comfort compared to not knowing whether he'd made it out of the doomed Earth at all. Even seeing someone in the mess hall pick up a spoon turned into, *I remember seeing Aaron eat soup that one time we did that double date in Newark right after he got into Rutgers.* Bill would roll that thought up tight and stuff it down his throat. He'd let it out when others in the shelter had the decency to pretend not to hear and turned their backs in the dormitory. Sometimes he used the bathroom stall, but the sound of his sobbing echoed.

Late at night on the fifth night, the police came. The one who took him had strong hands. "William Leary Warespoon?" He didn't wait for an answer. "You're being reallocated."

The city night was hot and dark, and the elevators rose and sank so fast Bill's ears popped. When they finally dumped him back at street level, he was wearing a wristband he couldn't get off. In the dormitory of the new shelter on a new copy of the same street there were ten of him and three of Aaron.

He was the last to arrive and the other Bills crowded him out when he tried to talk to one of the versions of his brother. So, he sat on the bed trying to listen in and didn't sleep until after the pale sun burned its way through the window.

When the noise of lunch preparations woke him up Bill felt a pressure at the foot of his bed as his bleary eyes focused. He saw Aaron's kind gray eyes smiling and heard, "Hey, brother." His eyes were bloodshot, and the voice creaked, and behind him, sitting on another bed, another Bill wore a bandage over a swollen, purple cheek.

I thought you were dead, didn't make any sense so, "How are you alive?" came out instead.

"Some of us stayed with you in line. The cops are dumping all the Bills and Aarons they can find here."

"You didn't get in the truck. You smart son of a bitch."

"I stayed with my brother. Just like walking the creek back in Teaneck," he said, but it was flat, worn from repetition. Aaron's chest rose a portion and then fell down hard. "I've got fifteen minutes with you before lunch. What do you want to talk about?"

And in those fifteen minutes Bill walked the creek with Aaron in his memory, and climbed the rocks in the woods on the other side of the hole in the school fence. Together, they picked up a rock as big as Aaron had been and they threw it in the air and watched it arc down to the surface of a frozen pond at the bottom of the quarry. Just before Bill heard the *wham-am-am* like God beating on a drum. A bell rang, and Aaron said, "I've gotta go, it's lunchtime," and made his escape without a goodbye.

Bill got up after him, following at Aaron's heel, but there wasn't another word, no matter how much Bill tried to start the conversation again. The quarry and the creek and the cairn of boulders all faded as Aaron loaded his tray with gritty mashed potatoes and turbid gravy. He sat with the other Aarons who talked amongst themselves.

Bill loaded his tray, ate hard, and tasted nothing. *That wasn't my brother.* But somewhere out in this city going on forever, his Aaron, or someone so much like him, must exist. Some Aaron whose brother Bill got separated and made a desperate leap and... *Died quick. I hope he died quick! I hope it was peaceful. It should've been me...*

Bill ate on his own.

After lunch, the shelter guards lined all the Bills and Aarons up and gave them brooms, mechanical grabbers, and a backpack full of garbage bags.

"Welcome to gainful employment," they said in unison, then they sent everyone out into the streets.

Live rats. Dead dogs. Rot. The streets of Manhattan had always borne a fog of piss and forgotten garbage and the Bills and Aarons lost themselves in trying to box it in.

A hundred and twenty, they'd told him in the shelter. It sounded great, except the shelter was charging a hundred and twenty a night for food and a cot. Five hundred days of labor for a ticket back to a living world—and that was if Bill stayed healthy, worked seven days a week, and kept his clothes serviceable.

An hour after Bill did the math, a body splattered a few feet from him. *Fell, pushed, how long ago?* Bill tuned that part out his mind off—finding a mental switch was getting easier and easier—and corralled the mess up as best he could. Now there was blood on his shirt.

Bill forged eastward for three and a half hours, prioritizing motion. Soon, he'd have to make a decision.

He was halfway across the looping map of Manhattan now. If he pushed on, there would be another copy of the shelter, *maybe.* He could swap places with another Bill, and the guards wouldn't care enough to notice. A different Aaron there, *maybe.* Maybe the right one.

If he turned back, there was the promise of pay and a bed and an invisible increment toward escape and a new life. Someday he might see a tree or a lake again.

As Bill pushed his broom along the Augean sidewalks of a New York City that stretched on forever in both space and time, a convoy of trucks rumbled past downhill, heard but unseen, carrying nothing on their way back to the world.

The idea Aaron was making his way out— had made it out already —never crossed Bill's mind. *The Warespoon brothers don't have enough talent to escape,* Bill told himself as he labored away under the setting sun.

Last Night © Gabriel Santin

COMMUNITY ORGANIZER

EDMUND SCHLUESSEL

I t was Fallon or Big Greg from the loading dock who started calling him "Little Bobby Lenin" when Robert got angry at every boss and shareholder the shipping company had. So, when the election finally came around the next year, it was "Robert Lennon" whose name was on the ballot, not Robert Laurinavicius. God rest his Lithuanian grandmother who would have died all over again if she'd heard! But politics was doing what you had to, to get what you wanted.

When Robert was a forklift operator, he would go to the bar after work and gradually surround himself with empty glasses. Once there were four or five, he'd start talking to whoever would listen and when he got some momentum people gathered around as he held court and read out rulings on everything in the world.

"Dodgers!" he said, waving a half-empty pint of amber ale. "I don't care if they moved to L.A. Why does it matter now? The Yankees are a million miles away back on Earth! They were my grandfather's team, they're my team too, and I like them for the playoffs. Not for the Series though. Whole National League, none of them can field for crap."

Or another time, "Green paint, green paint, why is it always green paint in the bathrooms? Doesn't make you wanna piss! Just looks like puke! Makes the smell in a toilet worse, too! Why can't they give it a nice coat of red? Red's a man's color. Bit of blood. Bit of fire. I'd sit in a red bathroom for hours if you gave me the chance."

It wasn't until Robert missed the interview to become a manager that it ever came out at work. He'd been just two minutes late; some delay on the M. Delays were happening more and more over the past few months as parts wore out and ordering new ones from Earth became less straightforward. Those two minutes meant they didn't even let him in the waiting room.

"It's not right," he announced to the whole warehouse floor, "when a man puts in forty-five, fifty hours of his life a week and gets no say in how his hard work gets used. What's fair about that?"

"It sucks," said Big Greg Paderewski, hauling a stack of wooden pallets on a handcart as he passed by.

"That's right! Listen to the man. It sucks!" Robert proclaimed. "We oughta do something about it!"

"What are you gonna do about it?" asked Little Greg Paderewski disdainfully.

Robert Laurinavicius found himself at a loss for words while the entire room was looking to him for an answer, so he said the only thing that seemed to follow. "We!" he said. "We...are going to organize?"

•

Robert skipped the bar and went straight home to find out how to do that. Pamphlets from the AFL-CIO the first night gave way to Mother Jones speeches the next night, and Joe Hill lyrics the night after that. The instructions in the pamphlets, speeches, and songs didn't say anything deep or original. They just repeated the same message: organize, organize, organize.

The next week on the warehouse floor, Bobby stood on top of his forklift in his coverall. Big Greg kept order on the floor while Little Bobby Lenin shouted, "We've got to fight!" and the workers said "Yeah!"

Bobby Lenin said, "If we don't fight, we lose. But if we fight, we might win!" and the workers raised their fists and shouted "Hell yeah!"

Robert Lenin shook his fists above his head and asked them all what they already knew: "Shouldn't we get paid what our time is worth? Don't we know best how our time is spent? If management won't give us a fair chance, don't we need to act?"

Nobody could disagree with what he was saying. Robert remembered a bowl of water he'd microwaved once, that stayed liquid until he'd touched it. Every drop flashed to steam, and he'd barely avoided an awful burn. Mr. Wizard on TV told him water could do that: superheat it, supercool it, it would stay liquid until something poked it. Then, bubbles or ice crystals could form. That's where he was, Robert Laurinavicius, at the point of nucleation.

•

The day the strike began, Bob wore his coveralls and raised the placards he'd painted himself, and the whole warehouse was so shut down the lights didn't even come on. The calendar said December but seasons were abolished in the Infinite Metropolis.

The picket lines went by fast. It took the company an entire day to send out e-mails firing the entire warehouse department, whether they'd gone on strike or not, but it felt like just a few hours. The police who showed up to haul away the remaining strikers, Bob, Big Greg, and Ed Fallon, didn't tighten the cuffs too much either, which was nice of them, even when Fallon took a swing at one.

They even showed restraint when Bob made a proclamation to the onlooking press. "You can beat us," he said as the cops hauled him away, "you can fire us, you can try to wear us down…but you can't kill an idea!"

There was another e-mail waiting for Bob when he got home, a speaking engagement in two weeks, at a fundraiser run by a charitable organization for laid-off firefighters.

Bob had nothing to do for two weeks except apply for jobs, so he read instead. "Look at this!" he told the empty room. "The workers elect delegates who form a sort of parliament, which establishes the working regulations and supervises the management of the bureaucratic apparatus. The management of other countries may be transferred to the trade unions, and still, others may become co-operative enterprises… This is how it's done!" His reading had been going farther and farther back, deeper and deeper into the fringes of radicalism, in a quest for... what?

•

As Bob stood before the crowd in the meeting hall two weeks later—observing the heaving multitudes of firefighters an d other wo rks under the cracked plaster ceiling—he felt his mind flash to ice. His notes were neatly aligned, but he glanced at them only cursorily. Now he was the great judge, thousands in his court, and upon his word, the world would change.

"Fellow citizens," he belted, "fellow workers, you may call me Robert Lennon, and I stand before you as a man brought low by the bosses. I am a man like you."

"We are all bound together not just by the callousness of individual businessmen but by the faceless machinations of capital. Brothers and sisters, I ask you, what has happened to the promises of the Deepening? Did not our Mayor, when he floated up to the sky in that balloon, announce an eternity of good jobs and cheap housing for all?"

Bob saw his magnetism reflected in the staring eyes of men and women, even children. When he paused, the room was silent as a tomb. When he raised his hand, thousands cheered. He tasted an opportunity like copper and zinc in the back of his throat.

"Now we live caged by the wealth of others, our escape stolen, as the wealthy slaughter us with impunity. Remember Ray Jilani and the refugees of Morningside Heights! Remember the adrift thousands of East Harlem!"

"And like Ray Jilani we have the choice to break from the cycle of our oppression. Brothers and sisters, I stand before you prepared to serve you. Tonight, I announce my candidacy for Mayor of this Manhattan—and I pledge to you, on the first day I am in office, this Manhattan will leave the grip of the financiers, this Manhattan will break free from its cage, and we will all leave the Infinite Metropolis and return to the world!"

•

Manhattan still had the legacy of New York in it, so the ballot had not just a D and an R on it but a C and a G and two L's. The sheer size of Bob's neon pink S among the throng put him behind a lectern at a televised debate.

"Impractical! Honorless!" spat the incumbent Mayor, his grey curls shaking. "We held a referendum! We made our commitments! There is no going back, and there is no space to argue with success."

Bob had learned glibness flowed like honey over audiences. "Mr. Mayor, sir, the scientists and engineers say there are no serious technical problems to overcome. Now, you talked earlier about honor, and then before that about growth...Mr. Mayor, can you eat honor? Can you eat growth? You've seen the food riots. You've heard how poor old ladies on the Upper West Side are dangling out of windows so they can find some space to grow some vegetables!"

The Mayor patted his hands against the sides of his lectern. "Mister Lennon," he asked, ignoring the moderator. "Mister Lennon. You use a lot of big words about community, looking out for each other. Well, isn't that true here? Our sister cities rely on us and we rely on them. How can you say we should abandon them? Ten years ago the people of this city voted. Two years ago they voted again!. Both times they said, we should join together and become part of something bigger. You and your fringe supporters would turn away from all that?"

Afterward, Big Greg took him to task. "You really oughta read the news from the neighbor Manhattans, Bob. Most of them don't like what you're saying at all. Maybe you should take a trip up east, see what people are like up there."

Bob knew the Mayor, slick as he was, had a point. Bob had gone from thinking just of himself, to thinking of his co-workers, to thinking of the little piece he lived in of a much bigger world, but nothing beyond that. He only had to win votes in this city—no other election mattered.

Bob knew he could count on a loyal core of supporters. Beyond that, if things didn't go as well as they could on Election Day, Robert Lennon had a backup plan.

•

Indeed, things didn't go as well as they could, by one and a half percentage points in a crowded field. Thirty-six percent versus thirty-eight wasn't so bad.

Bob decided it was time to return to his element. He called a rally for Zuccotti Park.

Zuccotti, in the sight of the great financial centers of Wall Street, had stayed clear of detritus since the Deepening with layer upon layer of outdoor platforms and lifts. It still held thousands, it was still a public space, and the older generation still remembered what had happened there at the beginning of the century, and before that how it had come to bear the name of a bank chairman.

Bob Lennon—"Laurinavicius" was a fading memory—stood at the center of a ring of tens of thousands, more watching from windows. Red banners, green banners, red-white-and-blue all swirled around him, and Fallon and Big Greg sat to either side. If the world still turned, Robert Lennon believed himself to be its axis.

There was no uncertainty in his voice or his plan as he spoke into the microphone. "Fellow workers. Fellow citizens. The forces of inertia have stifled us at the ballot box, but you can't kill an idea! Today, we will—"

Nobody ever heard what would happen. A new torrent erupted from the subway station: banners of purple, flags of brown, and amid it all, men with armbands carrying larger-than-life paintings of Robert's face.

The vanguard swung their clubs and cut through the crowd like knives.

Bob heard barked slogans erupting sporadically from the assailants: "Smash the impostor!" "Kill the Jew-backed traitor!"

Fallon, itching for action, pulled the cardboard from his placard; what remained was a sturdy two-by-four, ready for swinging. After it was all over, Bob never saw Fallon again and never found out what happened to him.

Big Greg ran for one of the police providing security. The officer simply shrugged, and Bob heard Greg shout angrily, "What do you mean, 'private land?' What does that have to—" before the screams of routed thousands overwhelmed the park.

Bob used the confusion to find a space beneath the stage and hid while he looked for an escape route. And as he clambered down the metal stairs, escaping his Manhattan for a new one, he thought of the signs the invaders carried, the anger and singularity of purpose with which they marched in rows, and he asked himself, "Suppose I'd gotten that job. Suppose I was an angry little man, someone who knew the world was wrong, but instead of being stuck on a warehouse floor, I was some kind of middle manager when everything went bad. What kind of man would I be then?"

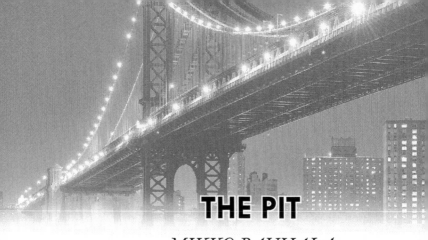

THE PIT

MIKKO RAUHALA

Consciousness hit Laura like a ton of bricks: hard, rough and heavy. At least there wasn't any light to exacerbate her hangover. What the hell had gotten into her last night?

Oh yeah. The Deepening. Either she'd celebrated the grand event, or she hadn't wanted to face it head-on without something to soften the blow. Or both. Both seemed most likely.

As the overall shock of waking up subsided, Laura started to become aware of specific issues in her sensory repertoire. A strong ambient stench filled the air. Besides that, she was cold and aching all over. A quick swipe of her surroundings revealed why: she'd been sleeping on concrete with some gravel on top for good measure.

The complete darkness suddenly started to feel less comforting. Where the hell had she lain herself to rest?

At least she was still wearing her jacket, and the one thing she'd insisted on was a jacket with proper pockets, women's fashion be damned. Her phone was in the inside pocket, safe and sound. She could get her bearings, even a ride home, but first and foremost, she could shed some light on the situation.

The phone's screen lit up, blinding Laura for a moment. She squinted and turned the backlight down a bit. There was no signal. Perhaps the cell providers had trouble properly adjusting their networks to work in the Deepened metropolis?

Slowly and carefully, Laura pushed herself up to sit. Then she activated the phone's flashlight. The dirty concrete walls enclosed a small space. The floor sloped toward a dark corridor at one end of the room. Piping dominated the ceiling, except in the corner where it made way for a hole with a ladder coming out of it. She hobbled over.

The way up seemed to be blocked by something. Leaving the phone on the floor for a moment to light her way, she climbed up to check. Indeed, the ladder ended mid-rung in solid stone, as smooth as ice.

It all started to come back to her. She'd been hanging out at a packed walkway terrace bar near Central Park. The park itself had been off-limits during the Deepening, but she'd figured the view would be better there.

However, all the alcohol mixed with the expectation had flared up her agoraphobia. She'd thought she was cool with infinities, what with her thesis on transfinite sets. In practice, though, she'd panicked when faced with the immediate prospect of staring into infinity, and literally crawled into the nearest hole she could find. This side of ground level the Deepening took on a more literal nature. Her agoraphobia would be the least of her worries in the foreseeable future.

Laura glanced at the phone. 19% battery. She cursed and turned on the battery saver and airplane modes. No use trying to find a signal down here.

She'd best explore her surroundings while she still had any light left. Laura ventured into the cramped tunnel, finding a passageway made out of metallic grill running through the center of it. At least she could avoid the gunky residue on the floor.

As she walked onward, the smell steadily got worse. Soon the corridor met a larger tunnel going from left to right. The walkway continued on her side of the tunnel. Laura thanked the far-away heavens for that. The sewer was full of murky gunk, and the surface was perfectly still, no sign of it flowing anywhere.

"Hello?" she shouted, her voice echoing in the corridor. "Anybody there?"

"Well I'll be damned!" a gruff voice cried out somewhere to the right.

Startled, Laura quickly gathered her wits and started running towards the voice. A couple of intersections and yells later she could see a flashlight in the distance. The relief was palpable; she was still trapped, but at least she wasn't alone.

As she approached the light, her cell phone revealed a shadowy figure. Bit by bit, it resolved into a dirty man in tattered clothes, his dark beard gruff and tangled. Laura imagined in other circumstances he'd have smelled awful as well, but here it was just par for the course.

"Um, hi. I'm Laura, and I'm glad to see you."

"Ha. Name's Jack, and there's a first time for everything. I guess it's nice not to be the only person here after they blocked every bloody entrance. It's like they're out to get me, personal like. Fuck if I was going to listen to their 'stay out of the sewers' crap; ain't nobody chasing me outta my home."

"Ah. Yes. Nobody," Laura said, nodding vigorously. "Say, if you live here, do you happen to have any provisions? Clean water, maybe?" Dehydration was hitting her hard.

Jack gave her a half-toothed grin. "Mayhaps, if you don't mind sharing a bottle with little old me." He swung his backpack onto the walkway and dug out a bottle. Laura caught a glimpse of a few tin cans before the backpack closed up again.

"Oh, thank you, thank you, thank you," she said, gulping down a modest serving. Then she returned the bottle. "Umm, we might be here a while. Do you happen to have more at…home? Or, is it just what you carry?" she asked with bated breath.

Jack furrowed his brows and stepped back a bit. "Well, yeah. Man's gotta be prepared. Ain't gonna show you, though, and it ain't gonna last forever anyway."

"But maybe it can! If these tunnels connect laterally to the other Manhattans, we could randomly determine which ones of us commit suicide. No, listen up, it's not like it's really dying since there are countless versions of us anyway. But then, the instances left alive could raid all the stashes they need!"

Jack's eyebrow had steadily risen while Laura talked. "That

sounds real well thought out, but no. I figure I'm gonna get to the Pit and get the hell outta here. The bastards may've blocked all the other exits, but it's not like they gonna dig all *that* just to block it again."

"The Pit? Oh. Right. I'd heard they did some digging at a walled off corner of the park."

"Some? They did all the digging in the world. Hole goes straight to the center of the Earth for all I know."

Laura's eyes widened. "Center of the Earth... God-damn! You may just be right! Lead the way."

"How nice that a simple plan without any of us killing ourselves suits the lady," Jack muttered and pointed out the way.

The pair walked along the passageways, the metallic clanks of their footsteps echoing in the tunnels. Jack took a turn to the left, then to the right, then to the left again. After five minutes of brisk walking, he stopped in his tracks and angled his flashlight upward. Laura hurried next to him and followed the light with her eyes. There it was, the Pit. It continued as far as the eye could see. Going up along the side was a flimsy-looking service stairway. Laura breathed a sigh of relief.

Jack pointed the flashlight downward. He huffed. "Better not look down. It's the same there."

Laura waved his concern away. "We have bigger problems. Since the pit is infinitely deep, it's astronomically unlikely that we, in particular, are within climbing distance of the surface. In fact, the chances are pretty much nil."

Jack sighed. "Well, what else are we gonna do but climb?"

"Right you are. If none of us do it, none of us will survive. If all of us do it, some of us will."

"You go first. I'll light the way from behind."

"Right."

Just as Laura's foot landed on the first step, a slowly crescendoing hissing noise from above caught her attention.

Jack pointed his flashlight upward into the darkness. "What's that?"

"I don't know, but..." The edges of Laura's mouth twitched upward. "I'm hoping it smells bad."

"What?" Jack asked, just as the torrent of fresh sewage from above reached them, its horrid stench assaulting their senses. While the waste had been piped in on the far side of the pit, a few droplets managed to splash Jack's face. Laura had put her arm in front of hers in time.

"Ugh! How's this any good?" Jack asked, wiping himself off and trying hard not to gag.

"Think, Jack! Where's the sewage coming from?"

Jack's face lit up. "The surface! We must be close!"

"Not infinitely deep, to be sure!"

"Nil my ass, then."

"Well. It's also true that a negligible measure of us were certain to find themselves high enough."

"I'll take it. Go on, get."

Laura started climbing, but her mind raced into calculations. What was the terminal velocity of the sewage? How quickly after the

Deepening had the utilities hooked the Pit up?

They might still need to stretch Jack's provisions to make it t
the surface.

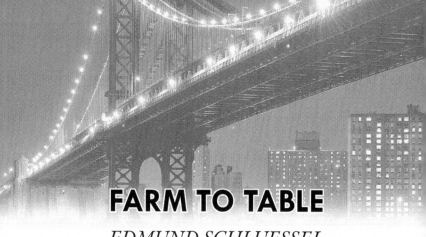

FARM TO TABLE

EDMUND SCHLUESSEL

Sarah and Jacquelyn rolled their beaten Ford Econoline through the orange-leafed hills south of Nyack, and as they crested a final summit before the roadway descended to the level of the Hudson, the southern sky glowed gold and red like the evil cousin of the Emerald City.

From the Palisades or the Tappan Zee, anyone could clearly see the confused vacant space where the borough of Manhattan used to be and still was.

"It's just a hole," Jacquelyn said after inhaling and holding her breath for a beat.

"Big ole' hole, yeah," her sister agreed. "Food goes in, money comes out."

"That's the deal," Jackie parried. She bit the inside of her cheek in thought. "You really think we'll get more than just selling to the canners? This is a lot of work!"

"It's just an hour. We'll see what happens." There was no answer to that, so the two filled the silence with Brooklyn radio as the remaining miles ticked away.

•

The food exchange in Englewood Cliffs bustled, and the Collett's little white truck swam uneasily among the automated behemoths hauling processed food in bulk for the Deepened City: frozen peas, balls of seitan, cans of corn. Every day, a day's supply of food for Manhattan, all brokered here.

The big sellers were all automated. Jacquelyn and Sarah inched their truck through the queue and waited for a human broker to come on foot. When he showed up, it was just a short, beefy man in coveralls with a databoard. He knocked on Jacquelyn's passenger window and asked, "what you got?"

"Corn," Jackie answered.

"Fresh corn!" Sarah emphasized. "Two hundred bushels of organic butter-and-sugar corn, harvested today." That last part was marketing, i.e., a lie.

Coveralls raised his eyebrows as he scrolled through his databoard. "Not a lot of fresh produce comes this way. Spot rate's one fifty a bushel, you want me to let it float?" He was posing as detached but already making a beeline for the back of the truck. Sarah hopped out to present their produce, outpacing him, opening the back doors to reveal neat stacks of unshucked corn.

Sarah leapt ahead of the broker and took an ear. She looked down at its neat rows of kernels, the end of the harvest, and found the pride that gave her sister the confidence to come here.

"Put it on the market," she said, facing Coveralls. Fresh corn in the real world sold for a few bucks a bushel. A hundred and fifty was trendy prices, and trendy people didn't know what anything was worth. "We can beat one fifty easy."

•

Inside Manhattan's food brokerage, money was flying as fast as the Bluetooth could keep up.

"Fresh corn!" shouted a banner-waving broker on the floor. "I have fresh corn for two thousand twenty!" That same corn had been bought for three hundred outside, wasn't even here yet, might be shriveled and dry—but nobody in there knew that. All the brokers knew was they'd started at five hundred and the bids just kept coming in. Twenty five hundred. Three thousand.

The price was cresting ten thousand when the broker saw a new face, a woman in white, approach him face to face. "I want your corn," she said to him, staring him in the eye, a Russian hint to her accent. "All of it. How much?"

Another person, a gray-headed man in a t-shirt, emerged from the crowd and shouted, "Twelve thousand!" as he rushed toward the broker. And as others came, it dawned on the broker, the meaning of the immaculately clean street clothes, the focus and single-mindedness of purpose.

The chefs were here.

•

A mile above the ground, the foreman checked a box on her databoard. The last of the day's food intake for this iteration of

71

Manhattan was on its pallets, and the orders from the one above them were ready to go. She was about to sign off when a flurry of priority notifications filled the screen.

"Why are they asking for all this corn?" she asked the empty air, swallowing to wet her mouth before phoning upstairs. Usually, communicating through a backchannel proved faster.

"Hi, Anirvesh?" she spoke into the phone. She'd never met her upstairs counterpart, but they'd talked weekly since the Deepening. "There's a ton of people wanting corn. Like, three times as much as we usually ship? What's up?"

"Some kind of rumor, Jessie dear. They travel fast you know." The rustle of Anir's beard crackled through the foreman's earpiece. "Fresh corn coming from the entry point, so everyone wants some before it runs out."

"And at these prices—" Jessie started to reply when she was struck by a thought. "Anir, you're a businessman. What if I told you I saw an opportunity?"

"Oh my," came the voice from the other end of the line.

"I'll hold up sending the corn up, you tell your floor we're fresh out, we wait a day and then tell the buyers they can go through us..."

The shock sucked the flirtatiousness out of Anir's voice. "We'll get fired! And sued! And...and probably thrown out a window!"

Jessie, meanwhile, felt bold. "We only need to do it for one day, hun. Then we take the money and run. Clear out of this city." She took a breath of stale Manhattan air. "You in?"

•

Laden shopping carts ricocheted against each other and the green-painted walls of the Safeline on the 9000th floor of the tower block at 112th and 6th. Shouts of anger; hatred.

A rush. A push.

A man tackling a woman in a muumuu to the floor, a can of corn rolling down the aisle.

The shriek of a wide-eyed child as his hand breaks between two rolling behemoths.

A gunshot.

•

"You can't do this!" Mrs. Derwitz shouted at the invading landlord. "The contract says we have until the end of the month!"

"So sue me," replied the burly Mr. Shaker. He motioned to the two large moving men behind him. "Take it all down to the M lobby. Anything you can't get in the elevator, out the window."

"The window?!" blurted Mrs. Derwitz, her blue-tinted curls lashing about in anger. "But...but...my bed! My sofa! You can't do this!"

Mr. Shaker looked down his nose at the widow in a mockery of equanimity. "Ma'am, I'm a businessman, and an opportunity has arisen to greatly diversify this entire building, making it more livable for everyone. This apartment has been re-zoned—for agriculture!" He flicked his soul patch in triumph.

Mrs. Derwitz, wide-eyed, mouthed, "Agriculture?" to herself. Did this have *something to do with the food shortages spreading all over the city?*, she thought.

Two more large men appeared in the hallway, towing something ponderous and organic by a shiny plastic harness. Henchman number three said to the newcomer, "Come on, around the corner," and gave the harness a tug.

The leviathan in the hallway emitted a long, lowing moo.

●

Chaz knew how to bat an eyelash, but Elmira was more interested in the view. "It looks like it goes on forever!" she squealed.

"We're a hundred miles over Central Park," Chaz intoned. "Look up."

Elmira caught the moment just as the piano player flourished. He knew the timing too: 5:55 PM every day, Manhattanhenge. The sun shone through the grid of the towers and lit every corner up with sparkles. She squealed again, shorter & sharper. "Oh, my eyes," Elmira said, and cast about for her purse and the sunglasses inside it.

Chaz took her chin and gazed into Elmira's dyed-blue eyes. "Darling, you look so happy."

Elmira bit her tongue without bending her smile. "Oh Chaz, I am! I would have never imagined such a trip." The sunglass case snapped shut loud enough to throw the pianist off beat. She slid the frames over her eyes and looked back out the window.

As she turned her head, for a split second, she looked down. Lit up in the visual purple of the glaring sunset, she could see the grounds of the Central Park she'd grown up adjacent to.

When she'd toured Edinburgh, Elmira learned about the Nor Loch, a natural lake in the center of the growing city that soon became a cesspool of plague, nameless bodies, and ordure.

The Scots had drained the Nor Loch and built a garden in its place. Manhattan had gone the other way.

Still, her lips didn't move, and she wasn't sure if they could sitting across from Chaz. Their dinner was arriving.

"Beefsteak with gold leaf for the gentleman," the waiter recited, "and sashimi tuna with farm-fresh sweetcorn for the lady." Purple against yellow on her plate, the meal sat.

Elmira had gotten a very expensive trip and a very expensive meal out of Chaz, and all her friends in Los Angeles would be jealous, but now the fun had run out.

She had a plan. Make a show out of eating the main course, skip the side dishes, fill up on wine, no room for dessert, the sooner the time to go home, the better.

Chaz was talking again. "Oh, that looks amazing, babe, I'd almost rather nibble on it than nibble on you!"

Elmira's reply was hollow, but it was still a laugh.

•

"See?" Jacquelyn said to Susan. "I told you renting would be a good idea."

"Truck's full," her sister replied thinly.

"Truck's going home full." The big robotic cargo haulers still stood in their rows, waiting for orders to depart for the Holland Tunnel and the hungry mouths of the Infinite City.

But there were rows of independent farmers in vans or tractor trailers too. Maybe one in a hundred would make a sale today.

The man in coveralls walked past, hustling from point A to point B. Jacquelyn knocked on her window, then lowered it. "Hey!" she shouted. "Hey!"

He looked at her, shook his head, and shuffled onward.

With the windows rolled up, the Collett sisters looked south at the orange glow in the sky. It would be hours until the field of vehicles broke up, and they could start their last trek back to the farm.

At length, gazing into the vortex, Susan spoke.

"Big ole' hole."

THE HANGING GARDENER OF BABYLON

EDMUND SCHLUESSEL

Etta Derwitz brushed the aphids from one of the leaves covering Anthony, her favorite plum tomato plant. The breeze blowing from her left was sweet despite passing through uncountable lungs.

She took Anthony's prize fruit in her bony hand and brushed it. It was ready to be plucked, so she hooked her thumb around the stem and tugged—

Anthony's legacy fell to her right and away, following gravity. Mrs. Derwitz watched the fruit tumble, a diminishing spot of red against the abyssal darkness of the streets below. "Hell," she said, knowing nobody could hear.

"Morning neighbor!" shouted a feminine voice. Etta grabbed her climbing rope and turned herself over, her blue-washed hair shifting with the changing direction of gravity, and waved. She saw the woman greeting her was already moving on Etta glimpsed the backs of a print dress and an overloaded laundry basket disappearing down the hallway. Mrs. ...Dalberg? Dunleavy? Whatever.

She took a swig from her canteen—switchel, a mix of honey, water, and vinegar that was the peak of electrolyte delivery in the 1830s—and started tending the tomato canes. She was bent over one of the plaster pots she'd hand-crafted from reclaimed drywall, her fingers following the curve of the cane from the side of the building when a bang from above made her look up. With a half-second to spare, she dodged a plummeting tomato from who knew how far up.

Another me somewhere up there fumbled too, I guess she thought. She usually didn't pay attention to the other versions of herself which she knew must exist all over the Deepened City. She reflected on Mrs. Possibly-Darlington. *Why worry about other Etta Derwitzes hundreds of miles away when neighbors barely even know each other?*

She'd barely noticed the Deepening. Life with her husband Anthony went on, half at NYU, half on archaeological digs, the two of them in their own little universe already that continued on happily in retirement. Then after the Deepening came Anthony's passing from a stroke and the outrage of being evicted. Etta looked around and pictured herself in the world: just another speck, a single person hanging by nylon ropes off the side of a building that went up forever.

She was a single person, contradicting gravity in a field of verdant green and luscious red.

She pictured the tomato falling forever from some unimaginable height, and it occurred to her: a falling tomato doesn't make a noise until it hits the ground.

Etta used a window on the way to the laundry room in the hallway outside her new, squatted apartment to gain access to the blank side of the building where she fixed plaster pots and grew vegetables.

But now the window was closed. "Hell," she said for the second time that day, in frustration, and in anger. Her neighbor Mrs.— Dal-dal-*Dalrymple, dammit*!—couldn't possibly have closed the window on purpose, could she? Mr. Boerg the landlord had thrown her out to open a dairy, but would a neighbor be that petty?

Etta couldn't really say. She'd never gotten to know her neighbors.

Now was a hell of a time to stop by asking a neighbor if she could borrow a cup of sugar.

The thought of *sugar* caused Etta's fingertips to prickle and her veins to clench. A second later, the alarm on her phone went off: medicine time was half an hour away (option B: hypoglycemia time was about two hours away). Her spider-sense tingling, she began to weigh her options. She looked up and down the length of the high rise: no open windows she could see. Could she climb down fast enough to cycle through to the next copy of Manhattan and hope Dalrymple-prime had left the window open? One foot every two seconds was too fast to be realistic when she'd have to drive every piton herself. Could she...could she fly?

No, you idiot, you can't fly, she scolded herself. What would that plan have been? Soar down to catch an M conduit between buildings, avoid getting hit by a train?

The M-trains reminded her of monorails, like the ones she'd seen at Epcot back when life in the future was all about hope and jumpsuits. She'd never had the ego to imagine herself a superhero: Indiana Jones maybe, but not Batman.

Then what the hell are you doing here on a Bat Hook? Trying to meet Cesar Romero?

She pulled herself up, scaling the building. There was one fixed point she could trust: the anchor of her rope, which she'd hand-drilled into the concrete. That climb was the only time she'd felt vertigo. Having the productive work of tending the garden put the fear aside: sure it was dangerous, but at her age, she might keel over as suddenly as Anthony had.

Any moment, everything could slip through her fingers.

Slip.

Slip.

Slip, went her right foot.

Down she went, free-falling until she could brake herself with her harness. Maybe fifteen feet? A fall always felt like more.

Etta scaled the building again with greater trepidation and caution, and soon, the soles of her boots were against the cool glass of her hallway. She didn't give the windowpane a stomp with her heel: physics didn't work like that. Instead, she leapt with both feet and swung her whole weight against the building, the head of a pendulum.

She bounced, scraping her knee in the process of coming to rest.

The windows were too thick. Her engagement ring was diamond, but cutting glass only worked in movies.

Options, options, options. Did the building have some kind of lobby? She faintly remembered one from moving in. *What floor do I live on?* Her apartment number started with 23. So, twenty-three floors down. *I can climb that much. A few hundred feet.* She began to play out her rope as she started speaking to herself, tasting the idea.

"I climb down two hundred thirty feet. There's a connector to the next building. I can get inside there. Then elevator home. Everything's fi—" A jerk in the rope interrupted her thoughts. Time for the next piton. She reached in her bag.

She only had two. Why would she have packed the dozens she'd need to climb twenty-three floors? She knew that. "The hypoglycemia's already here," she said, as her fingertips clenched again. "No, no, it's just panic, you're not thinking things through because you're up against a hard place." *Is that supposed to be better?*

Etta checked her phone again and canceled the alarm. She only had a minute before her medication was overdue.

She surveyed the walls around her again and thought back to first principles. The skyscraper was anything but sheer. Even now, her weight was borne by the sill of a long window. She could make it to the next window, and the next, until she reached the corner of the building... Then what?

Just before the lip of the building was a steam pipe. She had no idea if steam still ran through it, but it ran the building's height.

Could I climb down? No. Bad idea. Still too far. Might be too hot. Cooked Etta! Lacking a better idea, she started the sideways climb past empty hallways and abandoned apartments towards the edge.

She knew she had neighbors somewhere. Yet every apartment she passed was abandoned, some cleaned out, and some in disarray. All that space she could have had if she'd gone exploring instead of wasting her time greening the outside of the building.

No. It's not a waste. It's a signal. She pictured herself again, a speck against the building in a thriving field of tomatoes. Maybe nobody could see her, but as long as rain continued to fall, the denizens of Manhattan would be able to observe her handiwork for miles around. And when she was gone, even when she was forgotten, some future explorer would probe her exquisite garden growing amid desolation, and imagine the life of the hanging gardener of Babylon.

Besides, even if nobody was using those apartments now, she didn't want to be a bother.

Etta's left foot met air. She had reached the end of the windowsill. The pipe was easily seven feet away, damn all perspective.

She had one chance at a pendulum, or else cower on the window's ledge forever.

She pondered and contemplated until a slamming door inside the apartment on the other side of the window startled her. Etta scrambled for her rope, scrambled for open-air, found herself hooking the rusty, warm pipe with one foot as she dangled from her piton.

There was someone inside who could open the window, and Etta needed to reach them. Etta was a foot below the window; someone looking out would never see her. She had her hammer for driving the pitons, and now the pipe was within her reach.

And she had options. Did she want to try her luck downclimbing, hoping she could make it to some notional lobby?

Did she want to try her luck failing to downclimb, and never have to worry about her medicine or her aching back or missing her husband ever again?

She thought of Anthony and EPOCT in Florida and the rising sun. Then, she raised her hammer and knocked twice on the pipe.

Etta's arm was heavy as lead. She felt fire in her legs as her muscles revolted. Easy to say she'd tried and give up. She fought her fatigue and swung the hammer again.

Regular raps of metal against metal, but not too regular. It would let whoever's was inside know there was something more than a chrome-domed pigeon outside.

Etta banged away with aplomb, grunting with exertion. The racket drowning out all else, including the squeak of window hinges.

"Who are you?" asked a boy about seven, spiky-haired under a faded Yankees baseball cap. He was looking straight at Etta, straight down, but didn't flinch at the height as he leaned out the open window.

Etta flushed as if caught doing something taboo. "Hehe—why, hello, young man! I'm Mrs. Derwitz, from down the hall."

"Mommy says I'm not supposed to let strangers in," he said, cutting to the chase.

Etta couldn't blame him. Any city, especially a Deepened one, was an unknown quantity. "Son," she replied, sugar-sweet over a lemony center, "I'm eighty-years-old, and this is an emergency. Can I come in?"

His name was Rudy, and he liked lizards. It turned out he also hated switchel, but that was only sensible.

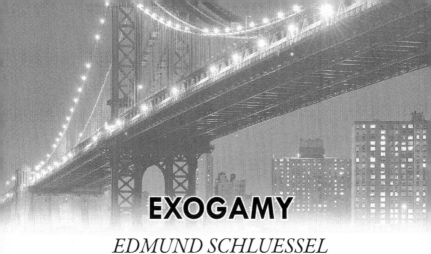

EXOGAMY

EDMUND SCHLUESSEL

Amsterdam Avenue at MLK Boulevard. Ray, Ray, and Henske stood at the corner and looked north. Across the way was a new Manhattan with the Holland Tunnel beckoning beyond.

There was no traffic. Henske pushed the button on the crosswalk.

"C'mon!" admonished Famous Original Ray. "You know the buttons don't do shit!" It was daytime, and the streets were empty anyway. The trio hadn't seen a food hauler for hours. Sometimes an M train would rattle from overhead in the distance. The only other sound in the empty streets was the rustling of brown leaves in a dying corner park.

"Fine. I'll just cross." The worn heels of Henske's flats shuffled across the pavement as she rushed in a huff. As she passed the half-way point in the street, a crossing light changed from white to a dark red "N'T WALK," the D and O obliterated by tiny circles.

Henske's blue jeans were developing an unfortunate tear in the seat, and Famous Original Ray spent a few seconds simply watching Henske cross. Ray saw where his doppelgänger's's eyes were aimed and glared at Famous Original Ray with contempt and jealousy.

"Classy, bro," he said while stealing a glance. It wasn't his fault; he was the second Ray from the bottom, not the first. God playing dice was the only reason Famous Original Ray heard Henske's pleas for help first, had gotten to the street first.

"You and a million others would look too, bro," Famous Original Ray replied. Where were the others, anyway? Maybe they'd just never heard that voice at the threshold of detectability a few days.

Or maybe they couldn't find Ray and Ray and Henske in the mounds of detritus and shit piling up all around them. The streets of Manhattan were on their way out as a home for civilized life. Ray smelled a million miles of breeze, bearing with it every fart, cigarette puff, and leftover Chinese food carton stink from a neverending civilization over his head. These had been low-rise apartments, before the building flurry leading up to the Deepening. Now they were like the tenements of his great-great-grandparents' day: built fast and cheap, without regard for the people inside.

By the standards of this part of Manhattan, the Wall Street towers ahead of Ray were old, the octahedral Freedom Tower having risen in his youth.

Famous Original Ray nodded toward his copy and said, "Come on." He started across the tarmac.

Ray sucked on his cigarette—still plenty left—and waited to finish it. Famous Original Ray halted in his steps and fell and a blotch of red spread across the back of his blue button-down work shirt. Sound slower than light reached Ray's ear a flicker later from off to the left, out of the dying forest.

Famous Original Ray wasn't moving as Ray sprinted into the street.

"Ray!" he shouted as he ran when he felt a sting in his own flank, then a deeper pain, throbbing and dulling. The world around him lost color as he sank. Far away, Henske was screaming. He heard his own name, or maybe she was calling for his copy? Then his consciousness faded.

•

A Manhattan away, Ray sucked on his cigarette—still plenty left— and waited to finish it. Famous Original Ray leapt up and fell and a blotch of red tore across his jeans and down his leg. Sound slower than light reached Ray's ear a flicker later from off to the left, out of the dying forest.

Famous Original Ray was twitching in shock as Ray sprinted into the street.

"Ray!" he shouted as he ran, when he felt hot metal bite into his shoulder, then a peppering of needles down his spine. The world around him lost color as he sank. Far away, Henske was screaming. He heard his own name, or maybe she was calling for his copy? Then his consciousness faded.

•

A Manhattan away, Ray sucked on his cigarette—still plenty left— and waited to finish it. Famous Original Ray's head exploded like a melon under a sledgehammer. Sound slower than light reached Ray's ear a flicker later from off to the left, out of the dying forest.

Famous Original Ray was clearly beyond help as Ray sprinted into the street.

"Ray!" he shouted as he ran when he felt a blow to the side of his own head. Perception scrambled and pieces of the world disappeared. Ray fell face-first on the pavement and tasted his own blood. Far away, a woman was screaming. He heard sounds he felt like he should recognize. Then his consciousness disintegrated.

•

A Manhattan away, Ray sucked on his cigarette—still plenty left— and waited to finish it. Famous Original Ray froze mid-step as a bullet blew open the base of his spine. Sound slower than light reached Ray's ear a flicker later from off to the left, out of the dying forest.

Famous Original Ray never had a chance. The gunner gave him the unasked mercy of a *coup de grâce.*

"Ray!" Ray shouted as he ran into the street, thinking to himself *this is dumb, this is dumb* even as he sprinted. Just feet away, Henske was screaming Ray's name. Ray scratched his knees as he sank to try to take hold of Famous Original Ray's body. The chatter of machine gun bullets had stopped—but now a rifle shot cracked the pavement by Ray. He did the sensible thing and bolted, taking shelter around the corner of a pharmacy next to the now white-faced Henske. He had his own backpack. No chance to go back for Famous Original Ray's. Henske took Ray's wrist and pointed up the street, into the

Financial District. Ray nodded, and together, the two ran north.

•

Tribecans. Damn. Tribecan *spies*. Cap Davis, "Captain Davis Meacham" to use the title the Morningside Militia had granted him that nobody really took seriously, waved one arm toward MLK Boulevard. "Why didn't you get 'em?"

"MG jammed," replied corporal Jarvis. "Nothing we coulda done."

Cap swallowed his frustration and looked around the squad, half of them lazing or chatting to each other. No wonder one of the escaping three had gotten across the street before anyone noticed.

Cap had slept badly. His bed broke during the night, worn out, jarring him and his wife awake. Now it was propped up on a stack of ancient phone books. His back ached, and he was in the mood to give his troops a kick up the ass.

"All right, you dogs, stand to attention!" The unfamiliarity of his tone roused fear in the troops, who, once the initial shock wore off, stood with shoulders square, but still facing every which way. "Six of you come with me. We're going into the Neutral Zone to root out those spies!" There wasn't a chance of catching up with them, Cap knew, but it would be a good exercise.

Cap nodded at the Financial District's shining skyscrapers ahead of him, where tiny gaps of blue sky peeked out. He led the way, and a platoon followed, motley rifles shouldered as they crossed to the next Manhattan north.

•

Every bad thing Henske had ever heard or thought about city life seemed to be true of Manhattan. She'd passed dead bodies while wandering from the hospital, trying to find some way back to reality. She'd even started to become immune. What had been too much for her was a dying dog, a writhing mess of ordure from the neck down, one shriveled eye still staring, staring, staring right into her...

The two Rays had been there for her when that happened. She'd started panicking, water rising in her eyes, and one of the Rays—she wasn't sure which and couldn't tell them apart even now—had taken her and held her close and pulled her away from the horror. Even in her panic, she felt how Ray was holding her a bit *too* close, pressing against her with something more than protection in mind, but Henske was resigned to the idea that men would never help her out of the pure goodness of their hearts.

She kept her eyes on the prize as she pulled the surviving Ray north. The Holland Tunnel, a way out, back to normal life. It was so close, even though every block and street was slow going.

Then the adrenaline wore off, and she realized she'd just been shot at, seen a man gunned down right in front of her eyes.

Nothing around the pair seemed to be open, even though it was midday on a Wednesday. The pharmacy looked locked up, the roots of buildings chained closed. Whoever came down to street level these days? These were the outskirts of the city. She looked up, saw lights in the windows far above her on the sides of towers tall beyond imagination.

Even visiting a place like Cleveland had made Henske feel small.

Her parents tried to give her culture, made her listen to the beatnik queen they'd named her for, but dammit, she even liked the smell of manure, in a backhanded way. Marrying a college sweetheart, settling down in a little town, a quiet life of accounting, it all made so much sense.

She looked Ray over. He was a weedy man, with a mustache that would never quite grow in. Strong, wiry, reliable, but nothing like the barrel-chested ladykiller who'd seduced her into this nightmare.

If Ray got out of this place, he'd be husband material for someone. Maybe cousin Judy?

Henske closed her eyes and reminded herself she was in shock. None of this was relevant. Get things back under control. No more fugue. No more wandering. Eyes on the prize.

"It's all locked up," Ray observed.

She nodded. "Let's keep going north. There's even less trash in the streets here. I think we can make Wall Street before nightfall."

Henske grabbed a granola bar from Ray's bag and offered him half. He shook his head. She bit into it—fake chocolate and peanuts—and resumed putting one foot in front of the other.

•

Ray, even as a lifelong Manhattanite, found himself disoriented. It wasn't just that the Battery was an area he rarely ever went to, or that the streets here disobeyed Manhattan's regimented grid. Space did something unnatural at the southern tip of Manhattan so it could connect correctly, and streets Ray knew to be curved somehow followed straight lines.

He and Henske wandered in wayward circles around Battery Park. The Holland Tunnel was just streets away.

"What do I do when I get out?" he asked, Henske hearing but not answering. "I gotta find a job outside. What's it even like out there?"

"The world just kind of went on, Ray. Nobody in Manhattan made anything the rest of the US wanted, other than financial reports. There's waiters out there…accountants…" Henske scratched her nose. "What is it you do, anyway?"

"I'm an office administrator," he replied, giving his stock answer.

"So what did you do all day?"

"I got paperwork from the City maintenance department and checked that it was, you know, organized. Then. I signed off on it and I sent it to the company maintenance crew."

"So…" Henske was gearing up for something. "…what is it you actually *do*, Ray? Like, what do you make?"

Ray growled under his breath as he tried to swallow his reply. It escaped, so he stopped and turned to face his companion. "You know what, Henske? I don't fucking know what I do! I get the paperwork, I sign it, and I never see it again!" He started walking again, towards what he thought was the edge of the park. "Same thing every day. Paper comes in, I sign it, and I get paid. This whole fucking city just goes in circles!"

"We're going in circles now, Ray."

Like she had any right to lecture Ray about getting lost? "You know what, I'm doing my best here, okay? This city is hell, and I haven't had a shower in days."

Henske sighed and lied when she said "I'm sorry." The next part was true, which made it hurt more. "I know you're doing your best."

Ray pointed to a building ahead. "See that? That's where the Indian Museum was." It wasn't, but it created the impression he knew where he was going. The pair crossed Battery Place, still exchanging insults until Ray felt a gloved hand on his chest.

"Excuse me, sir, where are you going?" said a pinstripe soldier, polite but with his leather-gloved hand grasping an automatic rifle. His hair was black, and he looked about forty, a porky white guy. His blue uniform was tight around the belly and waist, but pristine, with creases up the fronts of the legs and vertical parallel black lines breaking through a camouflage jigsaw of grays.

Manhattan survival instinct wasn't the same as most people's. Ray had no problem asking an armed man, backed up by rows of what looked like rocket launchers, "Who the fuck are you?"

"TriBeCa provisional militia, sir. Ma'am," he said, nodding at Henske. "What's your business crossing the Neutral Zone?"

"What the hell!" Ray spat, aghast.

"Ray, be careful..." Henske cautioned, but he plowed ahead.

"We're just trying to get to SoHo. Let us through."

"Then take the M, sir. This is a restricted zone," replied the guard.

Take the M? It never occurred to Ray he could. When he decided to escape the City, he'd committed to leaving his whole life behind. His M card was, as far as he knew, on his kitchen counter in his apartment, a world away. Rambling through the streets seemed right.

Nevertheless, with a glance from Henske, he surrendered.

•

Armed guards blocking the way into Lower Manhattan nearly had Henske striking north on her own, but she was loath to run away from the only person who'd shown her any consideration. A current of guilt shuddered through her over losing her temper in the park. Her feet ached, but she was angry.

Mass transit? They could have been out of this place days ago! No curling up on the curb, no street lights staring her in the face at three in the morning, no dogs.

No lead bullets smashing open heads and leaving unspeakable nightmares on the pavement, one eye open forever.

They were leaving the Battery to the south, and Henske hoped they were somewhere different from the intersection of MLK and Amsterdam. The signs across the sharp-angled lip in the street all said "Harlem," but the streets were as empty as they were historic.

She was willing herself not to look down the street, squeezing her eyes closed as she lunged ahead, ready to break into a run. Ray's even footsteps behind her gave rhythm to her own.

Then there were new footsteps, and Henske's legs pushed under her, leaping forward, not fast enough. A strange hand had her wrist, and she heard Ray exclaiming as she tried to get her bearings. Then, she was in handcuffs.

•

Cap caught up with the two squad members who'd grabbed the

spies minutes after their apprehension. Fuel was scarce but actually capturing someone was an emergency meriting use of his scooter.

They were a wiry man in a blue shirt and a woman in a torn floral dress. The soldiers were keeping them from talking but Cap's first impression was of civilians, the woman retreating into herself and the man performing bravado.

He didn't feel bad about the one they'd shot. Whoever they were, they were out of place. People in motion had started this whole mess.

He nudged the woman with his boot. "Hey. You. Name?"

She had her hands wrapped around her knees on the sidewalk, staring straight ahead, but with a start she looked up. "Um. Henske. Henske Maher. I'm from Shirlington, Kansas."

"And you?" He pointed at the man.

"Ray Jilani. She's not from around here. I am. We're just trying to travel. Just let us go, yeah?"

"You're an idiot for crossing a war zone, Jilani." Off to Cap's left, Henske burst out a brief, pained laugh. "We thought you two were infiltrators."

"You gonna let us go? Nobody told us about any fucking war."

That posturing...why couldn't he just make this easy?

"No, Mister Jilani, we are not going to let you go." Cap felt like laying it on thick today. "We are going to take you back and interrogate both of you, to figure out how someone so clueless keeps breathing unaided."

Ray struggled against his restraints. The man was lean and wiry, and might cause damage. Cap was glad the handcuffs had worked. He didn't think the squad had ever used any. "Take 'em back to headquarters. We'll figure them out." Sunset was starting to creep in. Time to head home. Make this someone else's problem.

●

Approaching the lines from the north, and expecting them, Ray could see the ramshackle army's positions clearly. They went all the way up, making a wall on the north edge of Morningside Heights.

"Does it go all the way...all the way?" Ray asked his escort, struggling for words to describe infinity.

"As far as we know, man, yeah. All the way up, all the way across." She took a breath. "Sometimes at night, you can see flashes way up there, guns, rockets. Down here, this is the edge. It's a real war up there."

Henske moaned, "This is ridiculous. What war?" Her own escort told her to shut up.

Ray took a leap of faith, banking on his escort's sympathy. "Yeah, what war is this? What's happening?"

The guard clicked her teeth. "You grew up in the City, right? You remember when the hipsters took over Chinatown?"

"Yeah?"

"Same thing. After the Deepening suddenly Morningside Heights was prime real estate, walking distance from Wall Street."

"There must be plenty of space. They built all those towers on the ramp up..."

The guard scoffed. "It ain't space, brother. A stockbroker won't live within a thousand feet of one of us. They tried to hike up rents to push us out, we started squatting, they hired a bunch of goons..."

"And you shot back," Henske spat, laughing again. "You city types, guns everywhere."

Ray barked back. "This isn't the 1980s anymore! New York is a safe city!" Ray took a moment for self-reflection. "Fuck," he said by way of apology.

The escort pointed out a station with an NYPD shield in bold blue over the entrance. "We're here." Ray felt the tug in his arms as his guard hauled him inside. "You got any ID?"

Fluorescent lighting blinded him after so much time under the sunset. "I got my liquor ID, does that count?" he asked, and the escort nodded before putting him and Henske down on a metal bench. They were in front of what used to be the sergeant's desk, but the man behind it wore a military uniform.

Ray sat in silence, counting the tiles, as he waited to be processed. The City had sucked him in again.

•

"Now I'm in a jail cell," Henske muttered aloud. "I hate this city."

Ray was asleep or putting on a good show of ignoring her. Henske still felt better than she had—the soldiers had let her shower and brush her teeth after an interrogation that was more of an interview. She thought she might even be tired enough to get a decent night's sleep on the cell cot if they let her.

But Henske's brain wouldn't switch off. She was afraid of what she might dream about.

She should never have told Ray about the other man. She'd hated herself for even thinking of an affair, hated herself for running off to the city, hated herself enough to do things she had never done before.

Shirleyville was stuck in the same loop New York City was. Drive out of town, and it was miles of the same farms over and over. Shirleyville was the same clients over and over, the same church socials—Henske didn't believe in much, but it was a necessary compromise to have any kind of social life.

She'd thought about kids. Toby would've gone for it, but she hated the idea of someone having a child to fill a hole in their lives. Let kids live for themselves. She had to admit her parents gave her that much.

She felt like she'd wasted the chance, but she couldn't see what else she could have done. She'd picked her major to guarantee a steady job. She'd married for love but settled down in a small town for security.

That was the trap, wasn't it? That was what they promised people who stayed in the Deepened City: steady jobs forever, easy to find a place to live...forever

Get yourself stuck in a loop. The City goes on forever.

Maybe it wasn't her that was the problem.

•

A few hours later, sleep evaded Ray, but for a good reason: the building around them was shaking from an explosion, chunks of plaster the size of quarters raining down from the ceiling. Henske jumped to her feet, then crawled under the cot for protection; Ray decided it was a good idea and hid under his own.

"What's happening?" she shouted over the ringing alarms, more angry than afraid.

"I dunno, we're in a war zone, so maybe, like, a war?" Ray hated being woken up. "Just sit tight. Nothing we can do."

"We've got to get out of here! What if the building falls down?"

Ray was pretty sure Henske could keep a falling building up just by glaring at it, but it was a reasonable question for someone from the country to ask. "It don't work like that. When they Deepened the city, it meant all the, like, pipes and tubes and stuff all hold the buildings up."

"You can't be serious, Ray! The buildings *literally* go up forever! You can't hold up something that big with a couple of pipes!"

Ray shrugged. What was he supposed to be, an engineer? "I dunno what to tell you. There's a lot of pipes."

The shaking had stopped, but footsteps were coming—booted steps. Captain Davis and his squad arrived at the door, and Davis fumbled with his keys to open the cell. He motioned to Ray and Henske, but as soon as the two reached the door, soldiers handcuffed them. "We're evacuating this floor." Ray guessed they were still prisoners.

"What happened?" he asked anyway.

"Rockets from TriBeCa. They blew clear through the building, around the 30th floor. They know this is the headquarters down here, but up there's just a mall..." Then too long a pause. "...Apartments...."

"They're trying to make the building come down on our heads," chimed in Henske.

"I just told you," Ray retorted over his shoulder, "it doesn't work like that."

"Not if they shoot out the building higher up!" she immediately replied.

Davis rallied his soldiers into action. "You two are coming with us. We're going to evacuate as much of the building as we can." Squad members hustled Ray and Henske out the door, as they moved in a horde towards street exit.

"I don't understand," asked Ray. "Everyone can hear the alarms! Everyone knows they should get out…"

The soldier hauling him, grim-faced, had an answer. "Cap and his wife live up on the 42nd floor. I think they've got a dog too."

•

Cap had the squad take the elevator in the next building up to the 51st floor—that was the first express stop—and then clamber across the connecting tunnel on 49. Each soldier took a floor and Cap led the prisoners to the 42nd himself. Once the rest of his squad was out of sight, he let them out of their handcuffs.

"You two are gonna help me clear this floor, yeah?" He'd radioed higher up in the elevator. If TriBeCa really was trying to slice off a chunk of this building and drop it on the bottom floors, the highest those rocket launchers the forward positions had spotted could hit was the 60th floor. That gave him a window, and maybe twenty minutes before TriBeCa fired their next salvo. His next call, to his wife, hadn't gone through—enemy jamming or the network jamming itself up as the entire world phoned. Who could say, in this mess? War turned everything into chaos.

Most of the apartment doors were wide open but he still searched methodically, making sure everyone was clear. One deaf woman didn't have her hearing aid on but came to the door when he rang her bell. He motioned her to get out. Ray and Henske were alternating apartments on the other side of the hall. He was glad he'd gone with his gut: nobody dressed that slovenly could be a TriBeCan.

Enough keeping up appearances: 4230 was his own apartment. Tension flew out of him as he saw the door was open. His wife had taken a bag, and Rusty's dish was as gone as the dog himself.

He grabbed a few possessions, a book of photos and a stack of rare coins, and threw them in a backpack.

As he reached the door, the world started shaking.

•

Henske was giving serious thought to running away, leaving Ray and everything else behind. A soldier might see her and stop her...she didn't know the way...she'd be all alone in this nightmare city...

She owed Ray a way out. That was the least she could do for the one person (two people?) who'd heard her and helped her.

Quaking. The bombardment had started with aplomb.

There were two M passes sitting on a nightstand in the last apartment she checked. Seconds counted, but she still palmed one of the yellow plastic squares and helped herself to a canvas shopping bag as she began to make her way out. She turned on her heel and she grabbed the other card, too. Then she ran for the stairwell.

•

Ray was alone in a Manhattan apartment again. He knew he'd been assigned a duty but he hadn't asked for it.

Ray was alone with his thoughts for the first time in days.

When the first rocket gave the building a love tap he found himself standing in the empty apartment, lit by the glow of outside street lights and the hallway's emergency lamps, and one foot followed the other toward the balcony. He put his hand on the handle to open the door to the outside.

Fucking door was sealed shut.

Everything that had happened since Saturday had been past some point of no return. Missing a day at work unannounced? They'd fired him already. He didn't have a place in this city anymore, except in the street, one way or another.

There was a lump in his throat. It would be easy to lock the apartment door, sit and wait. He turned away from the balcony and set one foot in front of the other.

Henske ran past the open archway.

Ray took a breath and went after her, back into the half-light. But he didn't run.

•

With the stairwell behind them Cap and his squad reassembled. The last of them emerged from the connecting tunnel, and for a second, seemed to sink as the floor tilted under him.

Cap held back a corporal from lunging for her comrade. There was nothing to be done. The beleaguered soldier slid backwards into open air a split second after thirty stories of building fell away, leaving a gap of open air and Battery Park beyond. Henske, to Cap's left, covered her eyes. Ray held her.

Lights were blazing, and beneath them, soldiers were marching.

Cap swallowed. He said to Henske and Ray, who stood uncertain among the squad, "They actually meant it. They're actually doing it."

As far as Morningside Heights had every known, the war was just posturing. The stockbrokers and the lawyers had to make a show they were doing everything they could to get the apartments, the tenants had to make a show they were willing to match them, and life would go on: an armed equilibrium, certainly, but an equilibrium. Cap could go home to his wife.

TriBeCa had spent the past weeks arming and training. They had thousands of people in uniform and in formation, heading this way. There were even armored vehicles, scrounged up from some National Guard depot.

He turned to his milling soldiers and the evacuees behind them.

"We can't win this. Headquarters will probably tell us to try. We could carry on a retreating action forever. All of us would die trying." A million times over, he thought.

"But the way to save the most lives is to get out. Spread the word. It's time for an exodus. As far as us low-rent folk are concerned, New York is done."

•

No retreat was ever really organized. Cap had found his wife and,

God knew why, Ray and Henske were still following him but none of his squad were. He was sure they were looking after their families.

The 145th Street M station was only beginning to fill up with what would quickly be a torrent of humanity. There were two options: south or up, and up meant the running would never stop. Break out of the loop. Even if that means leaving everything you know behind.

Cap had hoped his captain's bars and personal authority would get him past the M turnstile: city workers had developed a granite neutrality after the opening days of the war had blown out the skyways crossing Harlem and Battery Park.

But Ray had taken the two passes, scanned them each twice, and with steely confidence told the guard, "And them too." Henske and Lena and Rusty had passed through without incident.

A train rumbled in from the south—no balloon loop meant some creative switching—and the door slid open.

The closest stop to the Holland Tunnel was Canal Street. They'd be sneaking up on TriBeCa from behind.

If it was the same war as it was in Cap's Morningside Heights, the TriBeCans would never see it coming. If it wasn't a war...it was going to be.

FAMOUS ORIGINAL RAY'S

EDMUND SCHLUESSEL

Ray was grateful it wasn't just Henske getting out anymore. It meant a few more days together.

Henske had her ticket in her wallet, but the whole M ride down to Canal Street, Ray ruffled a few coins in his pocket. How much *did* the tolls cost now? What was holding in the pressure of millions of people in this place all straining to get out? When the WTC went down, Ray's mother had crossed the bridge to Staten Island to get out. Before the Deepening, sometimes Ray took himself to the Lower East Side, looked out over the East River, and seen Lady Liberty on her island in the harbor.

Ray had never sailed a boat, never even been on anything that floated but the Staten Island Ferry, but he missed the open water.

•

The refugees from Harlem had formed a camp all over Canal Street made of pallet lean-tos and cardboard tents, prompting the appearance of a ring of police and pin-striped militiamen. There were mothers and babes, people of every flavor. Some wore the uniform of Harlem and Morningside Heights, most milled in the clothing they'd had on: nightgowns and pajamas and robes. There was God's own queue at the exit terminal.

A few made it out by buying their own tickets. The moderately well off cashed in savings and dropped five thousand dollars on the ticket counter; the better off were in hotels waiting out their time for cheaper exit reservations in the future.

Ray didn't think he'd ever had five thousand dollars in his bank account at once in his life, and that was probably true for most of the people in the camp.

The camp was already melting away. Families drifted to find empty apartments to squat in. But as Ray walked side by side with Henske through the tents, he saw signs appearing, marker on cardboard: "Earth or Bust!" "We want out!" "Home?"

Henske had her ticket, but she was still there. She'd promised to stay as long as Ray did.

"Can most of these city folk even imagine North Dakota, Ray?"

Can you, went the unspoken question.

"How should I know?" How was anyone supposed to imagine a life they'd only seen on TV? "Besides, it's not just Manhattan or cowshit, yeah? There's Brooklyn, Jersey City, Bridgeport even." RThe concept of "Bridgeport, Connecticut" had an unwelcome tinge of exoticism to it.

"You should come out to Shirleyville, Ray," explained Henske. "Settle down. I'm sure you could find work as a...a...handyman?"

"Heh. I'm a paper pusher, Hen. I'd be as good with a screwdriver as I would with a machine gun."

"Back in Morningside, Ray, it could've gone a different way. Some other version of you's probably got a TriBeCan in his sights right now."

He took the little laugh that followed as flirtation. "I'm a lover, Henske, not a fighter." He smiled and tried to take her hand, but somehow it had moved out of reach.

•

Cap was arranging food distribution—people from the towers around them sometimes brought bread and canned goods. He had a tent and a stall where he made coffee and tea, and during the day, his wife would knit while he would sit and read.

He stayed out of the way of his former squad members. Since Morningside Heights, Cap didn't say anything he didn't need to. Ray, from a family of talkers, had a fondness for such alien quietness. He still hadn't talked to his own family, cousins in Newark, saying he might be coming. E-mail into the Infinite Metropolis was free, but they'd never written.

Henske hadn't written her husband either, yet. At dinner—thin vegetable soup in a big tin pot—she confided. "It's been more than two months. They said I had some kind of bad reaction, brain swelling. But to him, I just disappeared. He must hate me."

Ray took a breath and looked down at the wooden picnic table set up in the middle of the street. The tightness in his throat and stomach was back. He made a point of swallowing a spoonful of soup for appearances. "He'll be happy to see you. Who wouldn't be? As soon as you're in the door, all will be forgiven." Ray blinked. "Unless he's some piece of shit who doesn't deserve you in the first place."

Henske's cylindrical glass of water shattered on the tarmac. She finished her soup in silence.

God damn it, Ray, God damn it, God damn it, Ray, God fucking damn it, he said to himself in his tent under the humid, fetid sky.

In the morning, Ray was woken by the clicking of flat soled shoes outside his tent. He forced himself back to sleep.

By the afternoon, the only Henske Maher he knew in the Infinite Metropolis, and every possession she had with her, was gone back to the world.

•

Food riots were just rumors as far as anyone in Camp Morningside knew, but the drying up of food donations was eminently real. Ray had been skipping meals without thinking about it, but he heard discomfort in the camp rising in the chatter of parents lying to reassure their crying children, in the shouts from shop windows, and as September turned to October, as blue-uniformed NYPD officers raided tent after tent in pursuit of stolen goods. Many tents would never stand again after that raid, and one person would never walk again.

There was musk in the air, miasma, hot humidity like a cloak of gilded lead. Ray sat on the corner of Canal and 1st Avenue, not caring about the state of his blue jeans. A street sweeper carried on his Augean task in the distance. Ray, at the limits of his vision, could see a group of four in brightly-colored clothing flatten and flicker out of Manhattan and into the world: another happy family on their way, sailing on without impediment.

Ray only saw the end of a street. Manhattan had been his whole life, and for him, Manhattan had ended. He walked over to the coffee tent and broke Cap's solitude.

He asked, "What was it like, killing me?"

Cap took off his hat and ran his hands over his shaved head with a scratching noise; his hair was growing in. "I didn't pull the trigger, Ray. But yeah, I gave the order. You were walking through a war zone. You should have known..."

"I'm not angry, Cap," Ray interrupted. "I just want to know what it was like, and if it was easy"

Cap's eyebrows shot up. "Easy! Kid, before all this, I was a National Guard reservist. I never saw action."

"Not what I fucking asked."

"Let me get to it. I never saw action, but they had us train, right? Everything turns into a pre-programmed motion. My grandpa, he was a pathologist." Cap took a drag of coffee from a mug. "Used to creep me the hell out, the idea that he was cutting up dead bodies all the time. When I was about thirteen, I asked him, how did he do it? And what he told me was, there's this little switch in his head, and when he was cutting up people at work, that little switch would flip, and he wouldn't see the bodies as people, he'd see them as things, and he'd just cut things up all day, go home and never think about it again."

"I get you, yeah," Ray said, urgently.

"As soon as I saw you three, that little switch flipped." Cap shuffled on his steel chair. "Unknowns in my area, making a beeline for the Neutral Zone. That was it. Like clearing a line of crystals in Crystal Cram."

"It was like a switch flipping for him too," Ray said, nodding.

"Yeah. He went down fast. Didn't feel much. Over and done." Cap looked up into Ray's eyes, and Ray saw them sunken, falling away, shining. Then the soldier looked away again.

Ray sat down next to Cap, in the chair Cap's wife usually sat in, and rested in silence. It was morning, and the light shone from behind the tent. Ray could still see the vestiges of blue, starless dawn melting away on the eastern horizon. Cap served coffee, thin but hot, to the few who came to his counter, no more milk, not much sugar.

When there was nobody in the line, Ray found it the right moment to speak. "Cap, I wanna try to get some people through the Tunnel. Even if I gotta do it the hard way."

Cap slumped, dark brown lines suddenly standing out all over his face. "They're not ready yet, Ray. They're hungry, but they're not starving."

"Cops came last night, Cap. They're gonna come again. Mackie's in the hospital. It's only gonna get worse."

"And what are you gonna do, Ray? Get a couple of dudes to storm the whole thing with a gun in one hand and a baby in the other? Maybe it's time to start getting ready for something like that..."

"We're not gonna go up against soldiers. Just security guards."

Ray's certainty was growing, if not about success, then about action.

"The TriBeCan militia's security guards too, Ray. They've got money; they can train people up pretty well."

"If we move fast, we'll take 'em by surprise," Ray said. That was a guess.

"Ray, are you really trying to get people out, or are you trying to get yourself out?" Cap shook his head. "Look, I'm not in charge here; I can't stop you from doing something dumb. But can you give it a day and then we'll talk about it again? You're punch, I haven't seen you eating, I know Henske taking off has you all messed up..."

"Fine," Ray said, feeling his soul turn to ice. "I'll give it another day."

•

The next day was the day the world cut them off.

Nobody in Manhattan read a newspaper, but a couple of charged phones in the camp all delivered the headline: the City and State of New York had cut off refugees coming in from Manhattan. Ticketed passengers could travel, but the one or two a day allowed out as asylum seekers had turned out to be too many for whoever was in charge out there these days to tolerate. Ray woke up before dawn, having slept most of the day before, and as he sat outside his tent and listened to the world, he heard sharp anger bubble up over breakfast.

Weeks ago, Ray had told himself, *That someone is me.* Ray joined the line for breakfast and seized the moment, sidling up in line to Cap's old corporal.

"Can you believe this shit?" she said, slapping her phone with the back of her hand. "It's gonna take me months to save up." The tall, muscular woman had pulled the trigger on Famous Original Ray. That made her what Ray Jilani needed.

"I think we gotta do something, Charlotte. You still got your gun, right?"

"Shut up, Ray! People are gonna hear you. But yeah..."

In a few hours, with Corporal Charlotte's authority added to his initiative, it was a group—Ray stole half Cap's old squad right out from under him. He didn't like betraying the man, but, Ray reasoned, Cap had killed him, so Ray didn't owe him anything much. Once the platoon was together, a couple of people in fatigues with guns who looked like they knew what they were doing, people flocked to the idea: Ray and his little gang were filling a power vacuum. It was just six people with guns, and two-dozen others, mostly not spoiling for a fight, but ready to go.

When they were all gathered together at sunset, Cap came up to talk them out of it.

"I could call the cops on you, you know," Cap said, hands on his hips. "Have you all arrested. I'd be doing you a favor."

The rifles stayed pointed at the ground; it wasn't that kind of conversation.

"Cap," replied Ray, before trailing off. After a beat, he rallied. "Cap, you know I gotta do something, or I'll lose my mind."

"You're bored, Ray, that's it. Nobody's coming for us right now. We just have to be patient," Cap said, lecturing, "and we can do a fundraiser, or crowdsource. That's what Mackie's brother's doing, contacting all the other Mackies in the city he can reach, asking them each to put in a buck..."

"There isn't any other Ray Jilani, Cap." That shut the shaven-headed soldier up. "These past couple of weeks I've been online, phoning when I could. Ever since Henske left I wondered if one of them might have gotten out with her and you know what I found?"

"I'm dead, Cap. Some of me died crossing that street in Harlem. You killed me, Cap. A lot. But most of me...most of me jumped. Couldn't take it. If I hadn't heard Henske's voice that night, then I wouldn't have any reason to keep living, and most versions of me didn't. So I gave up."

Cap swallowed his first attempt at a reply. The new version made it out, "You're fighting hardest if you stay here, Ray. The bravest thing you can do is help."

Ray looked his opponent in the eye. "I'm not brave, Cap. I'm just trying to survive." The words tasted hollow in Ray's mouth, but it ended the conversation. With a motion, the improvised platoon and the families behind him shambled toward the Holland Tunnel.

They arrived in minutes: travelers parted like the Red Sea at the sight of the guns and fatigues, and plenty of people simply broke into a run. Even the guards, it turned out, were unarmed, and threw their hands up. The only challenge reaching the gateway itself, the elaborate and eldritch device which translated people across dimensions from Manhattan to the world and back, was walking the thousands of feet from daylight into the tunnel.

Ray had a little speech planned. He stared into the eyes of the woman in her Port Authority uniform and proclaimed, "We want to get all these people to Earth."

The woman looked back at him, unbroken but apologetic. "Sir," she said, "I can't do that. The City of New York has coded all transits. Without a valid ticket, sir, I'm afraid the system simply will not accept you."

Ray's gaze faltered as blood drained from his face, and he admitted to himself he'd run out of plan. He hadn't expected to ever get this far. The fact was he'd hoped to get shot before now.

The agent watched Ray, herself nonplussed. Ray felt tension building—scared people, some armed, with no way out in a confined space. He felt boxed in more than he ever had.

The agent spoke. "Maybe I can help, sir. I don't want any trouble." Ray nodded, assenting. "Gate controller, this is gate three. The gentleman would like to negotiate with you, could you come down? He promises he just wants to talk." She was a brave girl, and Ray turned to look behind him and in that second, he saw what she saw: a throng of skinny people in ragged clothing, carrying what little they had in shopping bags and disintegrating hand luggage. And Ray himself, at the front, scrawny and ragged and on the verge of crying for so long, he'd forgotten he'd ever felt any other way.

The gate controller emerged from a staircase that must have started high in the machine itself. No uniform on this one, but a Port Authority pin and an ID badge. He also sported a pair of wire-rimmed glasses, suspenders, and a bushy, curly gray beard. Ray knew the type: system administrator, engineer.

The controller extended his hand. "Jefferson Leakey."

"Ray Jilani." The handshake Ray received was warm but perfunctory: a solid grasp, one squeeze, and gone.

"Come up," said Mr. Leakey, businesslike. "I've been thinking about your situation."

Ray blanched again at leaving the group behind, but he'd put himself in this position. Diving deeper into the unknown would get him away from the pressure of being watched from all sides.

Ray followed Leakey up the stairs. They spiraled, through a narrow tunnel of metal, and Ray heard vibrations of every pitch radiate through the walls and steps. "I do read the news, you know," Leakey explained, leading the way. "Terrible, how there's no sympathy out there. I commute in, you know, every morning I drive down from Nyack. You'd be surprised what it's like out there without all the automotive traffic from the City clogging up the Palisades Expressway. I just glide right into Jersey City and park..."

The control room had windows, barely visible from the floor, but Ray saw the tunnel entrance, all the queued travelers who hadn't fled cowering in uncertainty behind the guards, and a flurry of motion at the tunnel entrance: police, setting up a cordon, pushing deeper inside. He hoped the soldiers had the good sense not to shoot. New York police didn't need any excuses to escalate things.

"Mr. Jilani, I have a proposal. As you might know, this Gate connects this version of Manhattan to its home Earth. But it can be re-tuned!" Leakey proclaimed, excited. "This New York has chosen to reject you, as have all New Yorks connected to the Infinite Metropolis.

But you see, in an infinite set, there are always possibilities...we can tune this gate to a New York of lower probability, one where, for whatever reason, a compatible gate exists in the Holland Tunnel, but with no Manhattan attached." Leakey even smiled. He was finally getting to play with a toy long sat on the shelf.

"It won't be the New York I come from?" Ray asked, curious. He wasn't stymied. The last attachment he'd had to his native world had left him behind days ago.

"You're just about the right age to remember the end of the first Internet, aren't you, Mr. Jilani? That was a great invention, one which changed humanity—and ninety-nine percent of the information on it was pornography. Before that, in my grandfather's day, it was rockets. Monkeys into orbit, then men on the Moon...and after that half a century of nuclear warheads. Every world-changing technology, Mr. Jilani, is put to use for the most mundane purposes. Marcie Kollan invented a gateway between universes, and we use it, not to explore, but to intensify and further dehumanize the way we work and live."

"Mister Jilani, I do not know what kind of world, exactly, I will send you to if you take my offer. But it is a world which could use its gates to make their Manhattan the Infinite Metropolis's problem, and they choose not to. So I put to you: such a world will be a better one than the one you came from."

A voice amplified through a megaphone rattled the room from outside, copied a fraction of a second later through the control room's speakers. "Ray Jilani! This is the New York Police Department. You are surrounded. Come out peacefully and surrender."

Ray looked around the little room. It had the look of a control room, to be sure: flat display panels, controls both touchscreen and analog, burnished metal. Yet Leakey had found places to install touches of humanity. There was a poster from an art exhibition long past, and a vase from which ascended a single yellow rose, freshly clipped. In a place of pride on the wall near a worn fake leather office chair, framed with the living yellow of polished maple, was a hologram of Leakey with people his age, and younger, and older.

Ray extended his hand. "I give up. You have a deal."

Leakey took his radio and called some unseen person. "Control to Security. This is Jeff. Tell the police liaison we've come to an arrangement."

•

Even then, most chose to stay and give themselves up. The scrappy corporal stayed by his side, and a few of the most desperate families, and a handful of people in as great a need as Ray were out. Negotiating with the police took hours; re-tuning the gate took minutes.

Everything came down, as it always did in the City, to standing in line waiting for something to happen.

The gate paused in the humming of its mysterious basso tune. When it resumed, and the lights returned, the melody was subtly different.

"Yo, Jilani," said the corporal. "You gonna look up another version of that woman you were in love with?"

Ray hadn't even thought of that. There *would* be another Henske out there—maybe one that wasn't married. He had a shot.

He shuddered as he thought of meeting her in October in North Dakota. The long fading summer of the Infinite Metropolis was coming to an end for him. "I don't think so. She has her own life."

Besides, the imagined idea of her would bring more comfort than the reality.

The gateway was open. Ray threw away the end of his cigarette and stepped forward into an unknown reality.

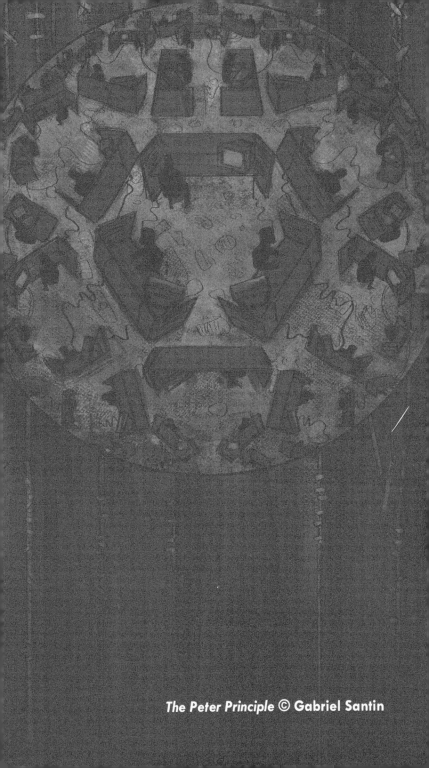

The Peter Principle © Gabriel Santin

ABOUT THE AUTHORS

Edmund Schluessel's short fiction has been featured in the anthology *Coppice & Brake,* in *Helios Quarterly,* and in Finland's *Tähtivaeltaja* Magazine. By day he works as a mathematics teacher, and uses the skills from his PhD in theoretical physics to give science and mathematics talks at conventions across Europe. An experienced political activist in the tradition of Judith Merrill, he organized Finland's biggest demonstration against Donald Trump and Vladimir Putin in his adopted home city of Helsinki. He tweets @stlemur and blogs at www.space-curves. org.

Mikko Rauhala is a Finnish SF writer with a master's degree in computer science. Informed by his background in intelligent systems, he is most at home in hard science fiction settings, though he's not exclusive and likes to cross genres. Whether the subject is steam powered gnomes or universal quantum suicide, Rauhala enjoys taking an eccentric premise and bringing it to its logical conclusion. As befits a Finn, his plot-driven narrative is often seasoned with a touch of dark, dry humor.

Rauhala has published nine short stories and a variety of flash fiction in various Finnish media, and he has a national Atorox award nomination to show for it. His English debut story, *The Guardian of Kobayashi,* is featured in the anthology *Never Stop – Finnish Science Fiction and Fantasy Stories.* He's also the co-editor of the drabble anthology *The Self-Inflicted Relative* and has had several of his English flash pieces published in other media.

CREDITS

TORI ANN MOTLOCH
ROCKY
CARL KIBLER
SARAH SIMPSON
AUROORA LAMMINLAINE
KATE ARILDSEN
HYACINTH BOKEH
LC DOUGLASS
JOHN LAMAR

Made in the USA
Las Vegas, NV
24 January 2022

42235128R00069